Arthur Tappan Pierson

The Crisis of Missions

The voice out of the cloud

Arthur Tappan Pierson

The Crisis of Missions
The voice out of the cloud

ISBN/EAN: 9783337339807

Printed in Europe, USA, Canada, Australia, Japan

Cover: Foto ©Andreas Hilbeck / pixelio.de

More available books at **www.hansebooks.com**

THE
Crisis of Missions;

OR,

THE VOICE OUT OF THE CLOUD.

BY

REV. ARTHUR T. PIERSON, D.D.,

AUTHOR OF

"THE GOSPEL FLOODING THE WORLD," "THE PROGRESS OF MISSIONS,"
"MANY INFALLIBLE PROOFS," ETC.

———•———

NEW YORK:

ROBERT CARTER AND BROTHERS,

530 BROADWAY.

University Press:

JOHN WILSON AND SON, CAMBRIDGE.

TO

THE BELOVED PARTNER OF MY LIFE,

WHO HAS BEEN NOT ONLY THE ENCOURAGEMENT,
BUT THE INSPIRATION, OF MY RESEARCHES IN THE FIELD
OF MISSIONS,
AND HAS INTIMATELY SHARED IN ALL MY PRAYERS
AND LABORS FOR THE WORLD-WIDE HARVEST,

This Book is Inscribed.

A WORD PRELIMINARY.

IF in this little book any good is found, it is, like most good things, a growth; it has come by a process of development in personal study and pastoral service.

The little interest at first felt by the writer in remote missions in regions beyond has steadily and rapidly grown. The logic of the Scripture argument for a world-wide evangelism is itself overwhelming; but various side-arguments and considerations emphasize and enforce the scriptural; and the logic of events adds its mighty demonstration, that the pillar of God still moves before His people. Under the combined influence of such an array of proof from Scripture, from history, and from experience, that the spirit of missions is the spirit of Christ, the whole mind and heart of a true disciple burn with conviction and glow with enthusiasm in the direction of the work of witnessing to a lost world.

Facts are the fingers of God. To know the facts of modern missions is the necessary condition of intelligent interest. Knowledge does not always kindle zeal, but zeal is " according to knowledge," and will not exist without it. A fire may be fanned with wind, but it must be fed with fuel; and facts are the fuel of this sacred flame, to be gathered, then kindled, by God's Spirit, and then scattered as burning brands, to be as live coals elsewhere. In vain shall we look for an absorbing, engrossing passion for the prompt and universal spread of gospel tidings, for full missionary treasuries or full missionary ranks, unless and until the individual believer is brought face to face with those grand facts which make the march of modern missions the marvel and miracle of these latter days!

To outline these facts is the simple, humble aim of this book, purposely compressed into a narrow compass, to catch the hasty glance of these busy times. So fast is the pace of missions, that, while we write the record, a new statement becomes needful; and so wide is the field, that a lifetime is scarcely adequate to its proper investigation. Whatever imperfections and inaccuracies appear, the indulgent reader will not forget that these pages have been written, only in the intervals of pastoral work, in a field where the exacting labors of pulpit and parish leave the pastor little leisure as an author.

The writer, himself deeply conscious of the defects of his work, sends it forth on its errand, praying that in some small measure it may prepare the way of the Lord, make His paths straight, lift up a standard for the people, or at least gather out the stones.

ARTHUR T. PIERSON.

2320 SPRUCE STREET, PHILADELPHIA,
July, 1886.

CONTENTS.

CHAPTER · PAGE

I. THE PRECEPT AND THE PROMISE. . . 11

II. PROVIDENTIAL SIGNALS 18

III. REMOVAL OF BARRIERS 29

IV. THE MOVING OF THE PILLAR 37

V. THE OPENING OF DOORS: INDIA . . . 43

VI. EAST INDIAN MISSIONS 53

VII. BURMAH AND THE KARENS 66

VIII. THE OPEN DOOR IN SIAM 73

IX. THE WALLED KINGDOM 80

X. PROTESTANT MISSIONS IN CHINA . . . 88

XI. JAPAN, THE SUNRISE KINGDOM . . . 95

XII. KOREA, THE HERMIT NATION 106

XIII. THE OTTOMAN EMPIRE 113

XIV. THE DARK CONTINENT 123

XV. PAPAL LANDS 133

XVI. MEXICO, LAND OF THE AZTECS . . . 140

XVII. SOUTH AMERICAN STATES 148

XVIII. THE SUBSIDENCE OF OBSTACLES . . . 156

XIX. WOMAN'S WORK FOR WOMAN 169

XX. THE PREPARATION OF THE CHURCH . . 184

CHAPTER		PAGE
XXI.	THE WHITE HARVEST FIELDS	193
XXII.	THE GRACIOUS SIGNS	201
XXIII.	THE TRANSFORMATIONS OF GRACE	211
XXIV.	THE PRODUCTS OF GOD'S HUSBANDRY	224
XXV.	THE ISLES WAITING FOR HIS LAW	239
XXVI.	GOD'S SEAL ON THE WORKMEN	252
XXVII.	THE ASPECT AND PROSPECT	262
XXVIII.	THE ELEMENTS IN THE CRISIS	273
XXIX.	THE UNHEEDED SIGNALS	281
XXX.	THE LEAVEN OF A NEW THEOLOGY	291
XXXI.	THE SPIRIT OF MISSIONS	300
XXXII.	THE LIVING LINKS	311
XXXIII.	THE PROBLEM OF MISSIONS	321
XXXIV.	THE LABORERS ARE FEW	330
XXXV.	MEETING THE CRISIS	343
XXXVI.	A WORLD'S MISSIONARY COUNCIL	355
	A WORD SUPPLEMENTARY	365

THE CRISIS OF MISSIONS.

CHAPTER I.

THE PRECEPT AND THE PROMISE.

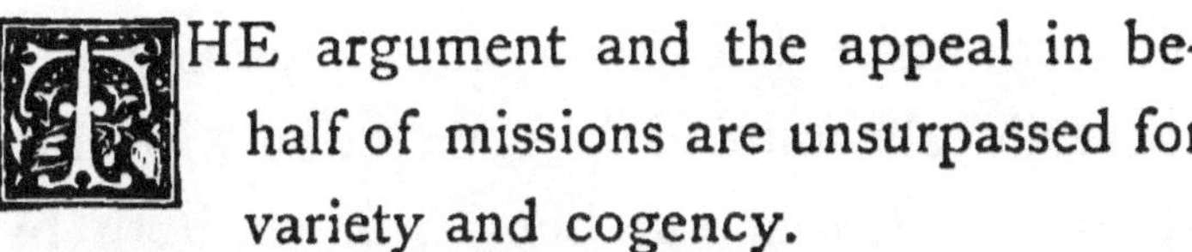HE argument and the appeal in behalf of missions are unsurpassed for variety and cogency.

First of all, there is the imperative voice of *duty*. The very watchword of the Christian life is obedience, and our great Captain has left us His marching orders: "Go ye into all the world and preach the gospel to every creature." Such a plain command makes all other motives comparatively unnecessary. "Whatsoever He saith unto you, do it." Where there has been given a clear, divine word of authority, immediate, implicit submission and compliance will be yielded by every loyal, loving disciple. Even to hesitate, for the sake of asking a reason, savors of the essence of rebellion.

When our great Commander left us this last precept, however, He annexed to it a most inspiring promise: "Lo, I am with you alway, even unto the end of the world." That promise has been conspicuously and marvellously fulfilled in connection with missions; for Christ has been with us, both by His providence and by His grace. The argument and appeal, found in this providential and gracious presence, have not been properly considered and appreciated; and we purpose to make them more emphatic by a rapid glance at the more important facts of modern missionary history.

We shall aim to show, for example, that the providence of God is especially apparent in missions, in the opening of doors, great and effectual; in the removal or subsidence of barriers; in the preparation of the field and the workmen; in the provision and protection of the laborers; and in the revealing and unfolding to the Church of His set times, seasons, and measures for securing new advance and success. Such divine providence becomes to God's people a glorious and inspiring signal both that He is always with them, and that His pleasure shall prosper in their hands.

The grace of God appears in missions, especially in working mighty results and effects, such as are plainly attributable only to the Divine Spirit. These results are wrought not only in individuals, but sometimes in whole communities; there are some transformations that deserve to be called transfigurations. In the workmen, also, whose consecration to such heroic labors develops in them an exalted type of piety, and even in those who earnestly pray and liberally give for the support of the work, similar unmistakable fruits of this grace appear and abound.

To these somewhat neglected arguments in favor of the work of missions it is well to turn our attention: for these providential signals and these gracious signs, being once truly recognized and realized, make duty a delight; the work of missions becomes no longer the cold necessity of obedience, but the most inspiring, enrapturing privilege. Only some such exalted conception of this last commission, and of the supreme blessedness of a loving fidelity to our stewardship in the gospel, can lift the church of God to a higher plane of praying and giving. Better than the conscience that drives, is the love that draws, to the work of missions. Once brought to the white-heat of passion for souls, we are henceforth "weary with forbearing, and cannot stay" in apathetic idleness and silence: the inward fire must have vent. It is no longer hard to give, but hard to withhold; and, better than the most princely gifts of money, we shall give ourselves, a living sacrifice.

These two classes of facts, then, will command our attention: the providential opening of doors, and removal or subsidence of obstacles and barriers; and the gracious manifestations of transforming power in individuals and communities in heathen lands abroad, and of reforming power in our church life at home.

Before entering into details, one startling and comprehensive fact should be clearly kept before us, — that all the stupendous movements and changes which we have to record, or refer to, have taken place within less than a century! Not until 1892 will the first hundred years have rolled around since, in that humble cottage of the Widow Wallis at Kettering, twelve Baptist ministers formed the pioneer English " Society for Propagating the Gospel among the Heathen." " Attempting great things for God, and expecting great things from God," they laid on His altar thirteen pounds, two shillings and sixpence, as their first offering for missions, covenanting together to undertake to spread the gospel among the heathen.

Within that yet uncompleted century what astounding changes have taken place! That bugle-call of William Carey has rallied all Christendom. God has opened the two-leaved gates, until the last of the hermit nations unbars the doors of exclusion and seclusion and welcomes to her ports the messenger of Christ. Even the most enthusiastic student of missions fails to apprehend and appreciate the grandeur of such colossal movements. Wonderful, indeed, that a hundred open doors, great and effectual, God should set before His Church; but more wonderful the ways in which, by keys of His own, He has unlocked the gates of hermit nations. And the rapidity of these changes is supernatural. When, in 1792, that pious cobbler of Paulerspury led in the formation of that first British society, and when, in 1793, he himself went forth as the first foreign missionary from English shores, the whole world was comparatively locked against missionary enterprise; there was scarce one real opening into pagan, papal, or Moslem lands to preach the gospel in its purity or win converts, without molestation and persecution both to the missionary and the convert. Now the whole aspect of the world is changed, and there is scarce one closed door, or community where the preacher may not go with the open Bible, or where the convert may not, in publicly confessing allegiance to Jesus, claim the protection of law. And yet these are but a part of the changes which make this nineteenth century the most conspicuous in history for the progress of missions. To appreciate this, we must enter somewhat into details.

CHAPTER II.

PROVIDENTIAL SIGNALS.

GOD'S ancient Israel were led by a pillar of cloud and of fire. It was dark, yet light; mysterious, yet luminous; obscure, yet glorious; instinct with divine intelligence, vocal with divine utterance. It was the symbol and signal of omnipresence, omniscience, omnipotence; the hiding of God's presence and power. Wherever that pillar moved or rested, His people were to follow or halt; and to move in its sacred shadow was to be guided by His wisdom, guarded by His power, and shielded by His protection. Before it the Red Sea and the Jordan opened a path in the midst of their waves, and Jericho's walls fell down; before it no obstacle could stand, no foe prevail; and happy were they who, watching that pillar, were always ready to obey its signal.

That pillar was a visible symbol of the providence of God, which through all the ages remains, to His people, the perpetual signal of His presence, power, and pleasure. We are to watch that pillar of Providence, march when and where it moves, and halt when and where it rests. In other words, though no longer accompanied by a visible sign or signal, to the attentive observer God is in history.

The Book of Esther seems to be placed in the canon of Scripture as a marvellous exhibition and illustration of God's providence, — that unseen power back of human affairs, distributing the ultimate awards to evil and to good, and by its mystic shuttle weaving even the minutest thread of events into the fabric of God's design. Some, it is true, would banish this Book of Esther from the canon, because in it the *name of God* does not appear; but there may be a significance in this fact, for it is a *hidden hand* that shifts the scenery, and thrusts the actors on and off the historic stage. This Book of Esther is the rose-window in the Old Testament cathedral, transmitting, as through stained glass, a light, dim, perhaps, but rich with divine hues; and by that dim light drawing attention to the exquisite tracery upon its framework and the symbolic design of its tinted panes.

So God is not less in historic events because the visible signal is now withdrawn. The eye of faith detects His prevision, provision, presidence, all along the line of the march of the ages. The devout disciple beholds still the moving pillar, and it is to him the perpetual demonstration of the existence of God and His interest in human affairs, and the perpetual inspiration to a life of self-sacrifice in holy endeavor and heroic endurance.

The argument from Providence is especially needed in this materialistic age. The prevailing ignorance and indifference manifested in the church of God toward missions prove that even nominal disciples are in danger of drifting into practical atheism. There cannot be a quick sense of God's being while there is so slow a sense of obligation and of privilege in respect to carrying out our Lord's last command and commission. Our first need is to know and feel that *God is*, and is the all-pervading, all-controlling factor in human history.

The main value of a careful study of modern missions is perhaps to be found in the unanswerable argument which it presents for God's existence and providence; and hence out of all those considerations, which blend in one mighty plea for the immediate evangelization of the world, we put this among the foremost. The logic of events demonstrates that the promise, " Lo, I am with you alway, even unto the end of the world," is specially and gloriously fulfilled to those who " go into all the world " to " preach the gospel to every creature." All the shallow pretexts for our neglect and selfishness, our meagre offerings and few laborers, are shamed into silence when our opened eyes behold in the history of missions itself a burning bush whose every leaf and twig are aflame with the presence of Jehovah.

It has been already hinted that a blessed inspiration is furnished to the workman in the mission field by this faith in the providence of God, and this consciousness of the divine presence. Prince Albert used to say to young men, "Find out God's plan in your generation, and then beware lest you cross it; but fall promptly into your own place in that plan." Dr. Anderson declared, as the result of many years' experience as missionary secretary, that "the great defect of the age is, that it does not respond as it should to the providence of God."

What guilt and folly characterizes him who wilfully, or even carelessly, crosses God's plan! What heroism and martyrdom must be inspired by the serene confidence and consciousness that one is watching God's pillar and moving with it! The true missionary must be heroic: he sees the pillar of Providence; across its white column he reads in Shekinah fires, " Lo, I am with you alway," and he knows that such a promise yokes divine omnipotence to human impotence; it means the removal of hinderances and the surmounting of obstacles broad as continents, high as the Himalayas; and he moves forward, fearless and faithful, facing foes as formidable as the giant Anakim with their chariots of iron.

But this matter concerns not only the missionary. Every disciple both may and should understand God's plan for the evangelization of this world. That plan is revealed in prophecy in unmistakable terms, and a close study of these inspired predictions will show not only the general outlines, but many particulars, of that plan. More than this, history is progressively unfolding, confirming, fulfilling prophecy. Current events are God's own commentary on his Word, and only open eyes and a docile mind are necessary in order to read and interpret them.

The knowledge of the Lord is covering the earth as the waters cover the sea. The stone cut out without hands has been growing for centuries, and is to-day filling the whole earth. That such predictions have a fulfilment on a much grander scale we do not doubt; but Christian history is full of anticipations and foretastes of the final consummation. Take a wide survey of the world to-day. No *figure* so colossal as that of the person of Christ can be seen through all the centuries,—even distance does not diminish its proportions or dim its glory. No *book* so colossal in its grandeur ever challenged the admiration of even the wisest and best of men, as the Bible. John of the Golden Mouth gave it its name, "ʹΟ Βιβλος," THE BOOK, more than fifteen hundred years ago; and the whole world echoes the name. No *fact* so colossal as Christianity has ever attracted the wondering gaze of men; it fills the world's whole horizon to-day. The foremost nations of the earth are not only Christian, but Protestant, and they have their grip upon the leading nations of the rest of the world. Prussia, England, and the United States hold the sceptres that at this hour sway the destinies of both hemispheres.

It behooves all disciples to awake and bestir themselves. God's eternal purpose concerning this world should be so engraven on our minds and hearts, that no doubt can ever arise as to the fact and nature of His plan, the destiny of the gospel, or as to our duty. Events are moving at such a pace that only the active disciple can keep up with them. This subject has a special interest to us of this generation, for we are living in the grand missionary age of history. Before the dawn of the nineteenth century, Protestant missions were so rare, limited, exceptional, as to form no marked feature of church life. In the apostolic age, the new faith ran on swift foot to the limits of the Roman Empire; in the mediæval age, the rays of gospel light touched here and there a rude and barbarous people, fringing with silver edges the dark, black clouds of paganism. But this is the epoch of *world-wide* missions. Since this century began, a golden net-work, glistening with heavenly dews, has been extending from the great centres of Christendom, with lines radiating in every direction, and cross-lines connecting, until the great globe itself is girdled and enclosed; the most distant and destitute will speedily be reached by God's evangel, and no land be left to the dominion of the death-shade. Theodore Christlieb attempted a "survey of Protestant missions." Awed by the greatness and grandeur of the theme, he was as one who from a balloon seeks to command a general view of an army so vast that no one horizon bounds it, because its lines reach round the world. What true soldier of Christ can be indifferent to the issues of such a campaign?

Again, this subject has a special interest to us of this generation, because changes more rapid and radical and revolutionary than in any preceding age are taking place before our very eyes. God is moving with great strides in His march toward the final goal. The gospel flood is fast rising toward a flood-mark higher than has ever been reached. The fulness of time has come, and the end seems at hand, which is also the beginning of the last and greatest age. God is specially working, and loudly calling His people to closer fellowship and more diligent co-operation. Such facts mark and make the crisis of missions. Now or never! To-morrow will be too late for work that must be done to-day. The time and the tide will not wait. He who lags behind will be left behind. Every day will make or mar the future of great peoples.

"The field is the world;" there are therefore not only many different points of prospect, but every part of the wide field has its own horizon. The march of the Lord is through the ages and around the world; everywhere the line of His march is radiant, like the milky way, with the marks of His golden footsteps, for the place of His feet is ever glorious. Where, in the treatment of such a theme, shall we begin or end?

For brevity of statement and unity of impression we select only the more conspicuous proofs of divine interposition, gleaning, like Ruth, a few handfuls from a vast and varied harvest field.

CHAPTER III.

REMOVAL OF BARRIERS.

WHEN this century was at its dawn, ten great barriers, to human view insurmountable, interposed between the Church and the fulfilment of the Lord's command. We may group them into four classes.

1. Obstacles to *approach*. There was little or no access to the great nations of the heathen world. China was walled about, Japan's ports sealed, India held by an English power hostile to missions, Africa impenetrable even to the explorer, and the isles of the sea crowded with cannibals more to be dreaded than the devouring waves of the angry ocean. In the Moslem world blind bigotry, as with the iron flail of Talus, crushed all freedom of speech or thought, and hung the death pen-

alty like the sword of Damocles over the head of every follower of the Prophet who even looked away from the crescent to the cross. In the papal world a nominal Christianity, intolerant of all evangelical creeds, forbade even the circulation of the Bible; there was less hope of proper missionary work among Roman Catholics than among Polynesian cannibals. Travellers could not visit the Eternal City without leaving their Bibles outside the gates, within which no Protestant chapel was tolerated. The Waldenses, in seeking to keep the pure primitive faith, found the Vatican an Olympus for its false gods, a Sinai for its terrors and thunders, and a Golgotha for its tortures and blood.

2. Obstacles to *intercourse.* Outward approach proved often no real access. Serious inside walls had to be scaled, even when the outer barriers were passed. Tediously slow travel and transportation made neighbors foreigners; languages, strange and hard to master, hindered even converse and commu-

nication, and, formed in the matrix of heathenism, offered no mould for spiritual ideas; moreover, at least sixty such tongues must be reduced to writing, having no literature, or even lexicon or grammar. Woman was hopelessly secluded within harems, zenanas, seraglios; degraded to the level of the cattle for which she was bartered, or the donkeys with which she was associated as a burden-bearer, unwelcome as a babe, untaught as a child, enslaved as a wife, despised as a widow, and unwept as dead, denied all social status and individual rights, and even *a soul*. Worst of all, caste, that gigantic foe of human progress, forbade not only conversion, but communion among converts.

3. Obstacles to *impression*. Some of the unevangelized races seemed on too low a level to be lifted even by the lever of the gospel; others stood too high, and were too proud to feel the need of its uplifting. In some not only the image of God, but the image of man, was defaced, if not effaced; they were dumb beasts for shamelessness and

wild beasts for brutality and ferocity, not only dehumanized but demonized. Others, like the hundreds of millions of India and China, proud of their hoary age, high culture, poetic and ethical faiths, and a social morality that in some respects put Christian communities to shame, were under the sway of a subtle priesthood, and clad in self-complacency as in an impenetrable coat of mail. The gospel might pass the barriers that hindered approach and intercourse, but here was another still more insurmountable. What could a feeble missionary band do in confronting great nations that boasted of their antiquity and aristocracy, and accounted apostasy a crime against both God and man, which was without apology and beyond forgiveness?

4. Obstacles to *action*. The Church itself had reared barriers to its own missionary activity. The disgraceful iniquities and immoralities with which the Christian nations were implicated and complicated made the name " Christian " a stench instead of a sweet

savor to the pagan world. England forced opium upon China, even at the cannon's mouth; vessels brought missionaries to Africa from Christian lands, and then bore back to those lands her stolen slaves; the Hawaiians caught the consuming leprosy of lust from the merchant ships of Christian countries; and the North American Indians took the infection of drunkenness from contact with our "higher civilization." The work of missions advanced under the awful shadow of a prejudice against Christendom for which Christian nations were responsible; for in some cases intercourse had already proved to pagan peoples worse than isolation. Missionaries landing on foreign shores were sometimes compelled to regret that the shuttle of commerce had already woven a bond of contact with the " Christians " whom they came to represent.

Beside all this, apathy and lethargy reigned in the Church. Ignorance of man's need and of God's work made the indifference that prevailed the more hopeless; worse than mere lack of sympathy, or apathy, there was, even inside the Church, antipathy to missionary effort; while sectarian jealousy checked activity, cooled ardor, and wasted energy that, with harmony and unity, co-operation and concentration, might have multiplied results a hundred-fold. At times zeal seemed to kindle, but only flashed into a flame of temporary excitement and contagious enthusiasm, soon to die down and leave no lasting results in self-sacrifice. Sheldon Dibble declared that Christians need conversion to foreign missions as really as a sinner needs conversion to Christ. Adoniram Judson said his "hand was nearly shaken off, and his hair nearly shorn off for mementoes, by those who would willingly let missions die." Albert Bushnell found no obstacles at the Gaboon so disheartening as those at home, in the "churches, one half of which give nothing, and the other half give little, but pray even less." No wonder if missionaries hesitated to go down into the deep, dark mine of heathenism, with no one to "hold the rope."

Such are a few of the representative barriers that, within the memory of men still
living, stood between the Church and the unevangelized world, defying all merely human
wisdom or power to remove or to surmount.
To-day, if not all entirely out of the way,
they are down, like Jericho's walls; and from
every quarter the hosts of God have only to
march straight before them, climb over the
prostrate ruins, and take the strongholds of
Satan. Nor has the half been told, or even
hinted, of the wonderful rapidity with which
God has done this preparatory work. It is
impossible to pack into a few paragraphs the
huge mass of facts which no child of God
can carefully survey without becoming a convert to missions. There has been nothing
less than a new exodus out of an Egypt of
apathy and insensibility, a new crossing of
the Red Sea, a new overwhelming of the
pursuing foe, a new pilgrimage behind God's
pillar. The angel of the Lord has gone
before the mission band till, within one century, its ranks reach round the world. At

the command of Jehovah land after land has admitted the heralds of the cross, till every people is now accessible, till in the most hopeless fields the harvest waves, and the whole aspect of the world is marvellously changed.

CHAPTER IV.

THE MOVING OF THE PILLAR.

IF the modern movements in missionary history have been under divine
leadership, we shall find the evidence
of unity of plan in the close and necessary
connection of its various parts with each
other. How is it? To him who carefully
watches the signal pillar, the conspicuous developments in the modern missionary epoch
are so related that each implies the others as
essential to one complete, consistent scheme.

For example, God has unquestionably gone
before His church to open doors great and
effectual for the entrance of the gospel. This
implies a corresponding movement within
His church to train and prepare an elect,
select band of warriors and workers to carry
the gospel through those open doors; and

these again imply another and more general work, infusing into His church as a whole a missionary spirit and imparting to it a missionary character, that the men and means might be supplied to keep the ranks of the advancing columns full, to preserve a line of communication, and to furnish the rations and weapons of war. Such have been the facts. These mutually necessary developments have all proven the work to be under the eye and guided by the hand of one Supreme Head. Whichever way we look, and from whatever point, at the history crowded into this great century of missions, we know not in what aspect of affairs these supernatural interpositions appear most wonderful. It is, throughout, "the Lord's doing, and marvellous in our eyes."

When we see a hundred barriers, that can only be compared to mountains, removed as completely as though they were cast into the sea; when we see a hundred doors flung open without human hands, after centuries of rigid exclusion even toward commerce, and leaving for the missionary an open path to the very heart of great empires,—it seems as though the miracle wrought in Peter's behalf, when the huge, iron city gate opened of its own accord, had been so often repeated in these days that it has ceased to be any longer a marvel. When we see how, during these hundred years, God has been leading out his chosen few to dare the assault upon the very citadels of paganism; to face without fear famine, fever, exposure, privation, torture, and death; and how He has made them brave, strong, and victorious, with every possible hinderance as to numbers, money, and worldly power, against which to contend,—we can only account for their courage, consecration, or success by the fact that He who went with Gideon against Midian, or Joshua against Jericho, has by His angel led this "forlorn hope." And when, once more, we remember how, one hundred years ago, the whole Church seemed practically dead to foreign missions; how Carey, in forming that first English missionary society, fought for twelve years the

apathy and even the hostility of his Christian
brethren and fellow-ministers, as Wilberforce
for forty years fought the English Parliament
to secure the abolition of the slave-trade and
the emancipation of the slave; when we remember that from almost absolute and universal indifference and even opposition, one
hundred years ago, the whole Church has
wheeled into line, declaring its profound sympathy with missions, forming its hundreds of
great organizations that ramify into almost
every local church, laying millions of dollars
annually on the altar of missions, and sending
thousands of missionaries to the ends of the
earth with its prayers and tears and blessing;
when we think that for the first time since
the age of the apostles the Church of Christ,
through all her evangelical denominations,
is organized for a campaign whose professed
purpose is a world's evangelization, — once
more, we can only exclaim, "What hath *God*
wrought!"   Only He in whose hands are the
hearts of men, to turn them whithersoever
He will, could have wrought such a change

in the whole attitude and aspect of Christendom within so short a time. Saul's conversion was not more miraculous than this new conversion of the Church. Here were barriers to the evangelization of the world quite as formidable in their way as any to be found in the superstition and hostility of pagan peoples.

But God moved *in* His church as well as *before* it. And so as we near the close of this first century of modern missions, lo, this missionary net-work overspreads the globe! Over two hundred and fifty languages and dialects are now the chariots to bear the wonderful words of life to the ends of the earth. What were rallying points in 1820 became radiating points a half-century later; and pagan nations, which at the beginning of the century were the slaves of vices that were eating away their own vitals, now, themselves evangelized, reach out a hand to help and save their pagan neighbors.

India is now a starry firmament, sparkling with missionary stations; Turkey is planted with churches from the Golden Horn to the Tigris and Euphrates, and the cross is beginning to outshine the crescent; Syria educates young men and women in her Christian schools, seminaries, and colleges, and from her consecrated press scatters throughout the dominions of Mohammed the million leaves of the Tree of Life; Japan strides in her " seven-league boots " toward a Christian civilization, and with a rapidity that rivals apostolic days; Africa is girdled, crossed, penetrated by missionary bands, and is drawing to itself the wondering gaze of the world; Polynesia's thousand church-spires point like fingers to the sky, and where the cannibal ovens roasted the victims for the feast of death, the Lord's table is now spread for the feast of life and love. Even papal lands now invite Christian labor. McAll crowds Paris and surrounding cities with his hundred gospel stations, and Signor Arrighi prophesies that the World's Evangelical Alliance will yet meet in St. Peter's Church and lodge its delegates in the chambers of the Vatican!

CHAPTER V.

THE OPENING OF DOORS: INDIA.

IN glancing at the opening of these doors we naturally begin with *India*, for when God entered that land with Christian missions He was driving an entering-wedge into the very heart, geographical and moral, of Oriental paganism, piercing the centre of the enemy's line of battle, that He might turn their staggering wings.

India was the " Gibraltar of paganism." It seemed impregnable. First, it had a great population — numbering then about two hundred millions — entirely hostile to the gospel. Secondly, it had two great religions, the most subtle, seductive, and despotic the world has yet known, — Brahminism and Mohammedanism, — and holding the people in an iron grasp. Thirdly, there was a system of social caste, that with the rigid, frigid fetters of ice that no sun ever melts, keeps manhood locked up, and prevents all social fusion and homogeneity, — caste that would make it a curse for the shadow of one man to fall across another, or for two converts to drink out of one sacramental cup. Once more, as though still to shut up India, even when the doors were open, the East India Company was there, nominally representing a Christian nation, really an avaricious, ambitious, selfish, sordid corporation, strengthening heathenism and weakening Christian missions. These were the four principal barriers to evangelization, all of them too great for mere human strength or skill to overcome. No man on earth would have been wild enough to have proposed the moral and spiritual regeneration of India, but for the faith that divine power is behind the gospel and the gospel preacher.

Yet India has been opened to the gospel, and the process reaches far back into the ages. Soon after the discovery of America, at the close of the fifteenth century, navigators successfully rounded the old " Cape of Storms," and called it " the Cape of Good Hope," and a new route was open to the golden Indies. In the very last day of the sixteenth and the dawn of the seventeenth century Queen Elizabeth granted to a company of London merchants a charter, the original basis of the " East India Company," for trading with the East Indies ; and in 1612 Captain Beal obtained from the court at Delhi sundry important privileges, originally commercial only, but gradually merging into a military occupation of the country. Factories became depots for goods, then forts, protecting the property and lives of resident foreigners representing the company. Every new foothold thus obtained was a pretext for new acquisition of territory and dominion on the part of Europeans. The growth of that English trading company in power and property is one of the phenomena of history. Seventeen years after the charter was issued the stock stood at above two hundred per cent, while the factories were no longer at Surat only, but at Java, Sumatra, Borneo, the Banda Islands, Celebes, Malacca, Siam, the Coromandel and Malabar coasts, but chiefly the dominions of the Great Mogul, whose authority had now set its seal and sanction on the company. In 1620 — the year that the "Mayflower" anchored off Plymouth — the capital had gone up from thirty thousand to four hundred thousand pounds, — over thirteen-fold in twenty years.

We refer in detail to the early history of the East India Company because this monstrous monopoly was the beginning of British empire in the very heart of the East. Behind man's selfish schemes, back of the avarice and ambition of unprincipled Englishmen, lay a divine purpose. Like Joseph's sale into slavery in Egypt, "God meant it unto good." It was the displacement of Roman Catholic powers — as represented in the Portuguese, who had exclusive privilege of commerce with India in 1587 — by the dominant Protestant nation of the world, which all unconsciously, and through the sordid instruments of a trading monopoly that hated missionaries, was laying the foundations of a Christian empire in the Indies. Meanwhile renewed charters with enlarged powers, renewed purchases with enlarged jurisdiction, greater concessions from the governments both of England and India, prepared the company for that new era which began in 1748, when the *political power of the British in India* opened another volume of Oriental history. Think of an English trading company, which could have been swept from the earth in an hour by the aroused millions of India, alternately expelling and protecting the Rajah of Tanjore, deposing the Nabob of Bengal, and, backed by British arms, compelling Tippoo Sahib to relinquish half his dominions and three and a half million pounds in bullion!

We have no space further to recite this romance of history. Suffice it to say that when, in 1858, the East India Company was finally abolished, and all its possessions and powers and prerogatives were turned over to the crown of England, its Board of Control had long been a court of final appeal. Its military force in the East Indies cost in one year ten million pounds to maintain; and the receipts of the home treasury were a million more. And the influence of this British power in India had been on the whole hostile to missions. One of the company's directors said that he would rather see a band of devils than a band of missionaries in India. From 1792 to 1812 religious and educational labor was prohibited. William Wilberforce led the movement which ended in a new charter for the company, providing for the *tolerating* of missions; but the change was only in name. Evangelism was hindered and heathenism helped; and as late as 1852 $3,750,000 were paid from public funds to repair temples, provide new idols and idol-cars, and support a pagan priesthood.

But in 1857 the Sepoy rebellion proved that the heathen, thus favored by the British government, massacred her subjects, while the native Christians proved her loyal friends, and from that day the attitude of the English government underwent a change: hostility gave place to neutrality and neutrality to commendation. In 1873 the Secretary of State for India put on record the following testimony: —

"The government cannot but acknowledge the great obligation under which it is laid by the benevolent exertions of those six hundred missionaries, whose blameless example and self-denying labor are infusing new vigor into the stereotyped life of the great populations placed under English rule, and are preparing them to be in every way better men and better citizens of the great empire in which they dwell."

The "London Quarterly Review" says of this report, that the "testimony of the Indian government to the importance and value of the indirect results of Indian missions is one of the most remarkable facts that can claim to have a place in missionary history." The fact is, it is a testimony extorted from a long *prejudiced and even hostile party !*

And so another barrier was down. If the policy of the government was still, in some respects, favorable to paganism; if "lands were assigned for temples and the support of idol-worship, equivalent to previous money-grants, and the government sinned in the lump enough for a lifetime," — it is still true that Christian missions were no longer opposed, but encouraged. God had permitted English influence and politics to become rooted in India by strange means; but one thing was settled, — the European power dominant in the heart of Asia was to be Protestant, not Papal; and so, in subsequent contests with Portugal and France, England maintained her supremacy, and the cross rather than the crucifix seems destined to sway this great Oriental empire.

Thus, by movements extending over centuries, the two hundred and fifty millions of India are made accessible to the gospel.

Five times the population of the United States there wait for the Light of the World to displace the fading "Light of Asia," and reveal Heaven instead of Nirvana. The door is open to the golden Indies, and in the whole history of missions no other such opportunity has ever been offered. Here is a colossal pagan empire, under one head, virtually controlled by a Protestant queen, and permeated by the influence of the great Christian nation which she rules; civil and religious rights assured alike to missionary and convert; with postal facilities, rapid transportation, and telegraphic communication; with sixty thousand schools and a hundred colleges; with presses scattering books, magazines, and newspapers; with the English tongue so widely diffused and so generally understood that Julius Seelye and Joseph Cook could speak to large audiences of native Brahmins without an interpreter. Here is the very intellect of Asia with its ancient literature, its imposing architecture, its vigorous faculties waiting to be won and then wielded for God. If India be the Gibraltar of heathendom, taken for Christ it becomes, like Gibraltar, a controlling fortress guarding the very highway to other Oriental empires.

CHAPTER VI.

THE door might be nominally open in India, and yet our missionary work prove a failure. Is there any reason to believe that the door is really open, that the gospel is actually impressing this great people? No country has presented a field of labor more unpromising. The general intelligence of the people, the subtle acuteness of a jesuitical priesthood, the prevalence of pagan faiths so fascinating that even educated men from Christian lands compose poetic panegyrics on "the Light of Asia," the seclusion and slavery of woman, the monstrous system of caste, and the strong hold of superstition on the common mind,—so many and such high barriers seldom defy the gospel as in India. They have dismayed even some courageous disciples. When Robert Nesbit was about to go to Bombay, Dr. Hill, his theological professor, said to him: "You must be a fool for going to India to preach the gospel there! Don't you know that the Hindus are all better than ourselves, and that by your going there it will spoil the matter?" And yet God has, in spite of such ignorance and unbelief in the Church, already wrought wonders in India.

A new population begins to make itself felt in India. Christian homes rapidly multiply in which the caste idea, which has ruled India so long and so cruelly, no more holds sway. To the caste Hindu these Christians are outcasts; but the outcasts are becoming so numerous as to form a community of their own. There are tens of thousands of them, and they are increasing more rapidly than ever. A silent but wonderful transformation is going on in that strange land, and is illustrating the power of missions.

Female education is making rapid progress, and is encouraged by intelligent and wealthy natives. A Bombay merchant lately gave fifteen thousand rupees toward the founding of a girls' school; and the Maharajah of Travancore has given a large sum in aid of female medical education.

Rev. Narayan Sheshadri, the converted educated Brahmin, is competent to speak and tell what he has seen in a quarter of a century in this most difficult field for gospel triumph. He says that an intelligent Hindu cannot avoid comparing his sacred books with our Bible. The four grand books called the *Vedas*, now, by European scholarship, unlocked to the popular mind by translation from the ancient Sanscrit, have had their mystic charms dissolved as light scatters mist at morning. They are found to consist each of three parts, — lyrical, ritual, philosophical. The lyrics are really prayers, and here is a specimen: "O thou Ugne, god of fire, that ridest in a chariot drawn by milk-white horses, ever radiant, youthful, come to our sacrificial feast! eat of the viands and drink of the soma juice that we have prepared." The soma juice is an intoxicating drink made from the soma plant; and this prayer is an invocation to a whiskey-drinking god! How long would it take an intelligent and candid Hindu to feel the immeasurable inferiority of the Vedic prayers to the Psalms of David?

As to the ideas contained in the philosophical part of the Vedas, they are seen to be equally in contrast with the sublime conceptions of God and of religion contained in our Holy Scriptures. It is not certain whether the god of the Vedas is one or many, or even personal. *Brahm* is neuter, an IT. For ages upon ages this great IT lies dormant, inactive; then begins to grow, till sun and moon become its eyes, the rocks its finger-nails, the forests its hair; and then it declares itself, I AM BRAHM! How what was without life, consciousness, thought, or emotion, thus develops, the philosophers answer by that convenient word "mystery." Here is nothing but an old, rude pantheism;

there is no human identity or responsibility apart from Brahm; man's sins, follies, and faults become GOD'S. What begins in absurdity ends in blasphemy. The education which by some was thought to lift the Hindus above the reach of Christianity is the very means of showing them the incomparable superiority of God's Word. Culture may not convert them *to* Christ, but it converts them *from* Brahm; and the most acute observers have boldly declared that Brahminism in India is dead or dying.

This is further proven by the remarkable decay of superstitious rites and practices. The *suttee* is a thing of the past: the widow no more burns on the funeral pyre of her husband; children are no more flung into the idolized Ganges by superstitious mothers.

Caste was thought to be the insurmountable barrier to Christianity; but the railway, that democratic institution, makes caste privileges too costly for the greed of the Brahmin. In the car he rides in the third-class compartment side by side with the lowest caste, because it is cheaper; and in the horse-car he does the same, because there are no compartments. And so Brahmin, Parsee, and Sudra not only travel in company, but keep company in travel, exchanging courtesies and converse!

Schwarz, whose combined manliness and godliness constrained the East India Company, and even the Rajah of Tanjore, to build monuments to his memory, sailed for Tranquebar in 1750. That same year four hundred were baptized, and in 1880 the native Christian population of India numbered upwards of half a million. There are hundreds of native pastors and native church councils. The increase is not simply in arithmetical, but in geometrical, progression. That native Christian population grew twenty-fold in fifty years, and during the last three decades the ratio has advanced from fifty per cent to sixty, and then to ninety per cent.

Not only is there this increase in numbers,

but, what is more important, in influence. To be a Christian is to be respected, to take an advanced position, to compel others to concede and confess superiority. Christians take the lead in intelligence, morality, integrity; the Christian home is a constant witness to the religion that lifts family life to a higher plane; the Christian church is manifestly a model of human brotherhood, the ideal democracy. Dr. Scudder, after twenty years spent among the Brahmins, declares that, though there is no keener intellect on earth than theirs, yet the gospel wins its way to their minds and hearts. Sheshadri turned from the popular, the philosophical, and the atheistic forms of religion to the Book of Books, and found more wisdom in the first verse of Genesis than in all the Vedas. Ganga Dhar, the Brahmin of Orissa, bowed before the Christ of God, and devoted his transcendent gifts and graces to the proclamation of the gospel. Even to those acute Hindus the logic of his head and heart is irresistible, and his simple story of the cross makes them cry, which is like "squeezing water out of pebbles."

Sir William Muir testifies that "thousands have been brought over, and, in an ever-increasing ratio, converts are being brought to Christianity; and these are not shams nor paper converts, but good and honest Christians, and many of them of a high standard." Sir Herbert Edwardes said, twenty years ago: "God is forming a new nation in India. While the Hindus are busy pulling down their own religion, the Christian church is rising above the horizon. Every other faith in India is decaying; Christianity alone is beginning to run its course. I believe, if the English were driven out to-day, Christianity would remain and triumph." Max Müller said to Norman McLeod that he knew of no people as ripe for Christianity to-day as the East Indians.

These are a few of the testimonies of representative men who have had rare opportunities to study the East Indian question; yet there are hundreds of others who give similar testimony. Sir Richard Temple, who had been a quarter of a century on the ground, and been governor of both the Bengal and Bombay Presidencies, said in New York in 1882, that if the growth of Christianity goes on at the rate of its advancement previous to 1880, "there will by the year 1910 be about two million native Christians in India." Sir Bartle Frère, in 1873, said: "Whatever you may be told to the contrary, the teaching of Christianity among the one hundred and sixty millions of civilized, industrious Hindus and Mohammedans in India is effecting changes, moral, social, and political, which, for extent and rapidity of effect, are far more extraordinary than anything that you or your fathers have witnessed in modern Europe." To the same effect are the testimonies of Sir Donald McLeod, once lieutenant-governor of the Punjaub, Sir William Hill, Lord John Lawrence, the Earl of Northbrook, Hon. W. E. Baxter, and others.[1]

[1] See Dr. Ellinwood's article. Foreign Missionary, Jan., 1886, p. 354.

A jubilee was recently held in Tinnevelly to commemorate Bishop Sargent's fifty years of service under the Church Missionary Society. He has now six hundred assistants, twelve thousand communicants, and a Christian community of five times that number.

But we are not limited to the testimonies of professed disciples, whose sanguine optimism might be thought to invest the work with a false halo. Keshub Chunder Sen, the founder of the Brahmo Somaj, records his significant confession that "the spirit of Christianity has already pervaded the whole atmosphere of Indian society, and we breathe, think, feel, and move in a Christian atmosphere. Native society is being roused, enlightened, and reformed under the influence of Christianity. Our hearts are touched, conquered, overcome by a higher power; and this power is Christ. Christ, not the British government, rules India." The Prince of Travancore, in 1874, said publicly: —

"Where did the English-speaking people get all their intelligence, and energy, and cleverness, and power? It is their Bible that gives it to them. And now they bring it to us and say, 'This is what raised us. Take it and raise yourselves.' They do not force it upon us, as the Mohammedans did their Koran, but they bring it in love, and translate it into our languages, and lay it before us and say, 'Look at it, read it, examine it, and see if it is not good.' Of one thing I am convinced, — do what we will, oppose it as we may, it is the Christian's Bible that will, sooner or later, work the regeneration of this land. Marvellous has been the effect of Christianity in the moral moulding and leavening of Europe. I am not a Christian; I do not accept the cardinal tenets of Christianity as they concern man in the next world; but I accept Christian ethics in their entirety. I have the highest admiration for them."

Thus even the East Indians themselves confess that before the gospel their own religions are giving way. Hinduism and Mohammedanism are losing their grip. Heathen men used to. say to Dr. Scudder, " Let *us* alone; our children are bound to become Christians."

Last October, during the semi-centennial

of the Basle Mission in Southern India, an address of congratulation was presented, signed by over one hundred residents of Mangalore, mostly Brahmins and all in high position, themselves keepers of caste, yet seemingly glad of the victories which Christianity has gained over it. The address witnesses to the high character of the missionary work in uplifting those who are educated in the schools, to a higher level, and raising the social condition of the lower castes.

It would seem not in vain that six hundred missionaries are sleeping in the soil of India; they are the buried seed of a coming harvest of souls. In one year sixty thousand left Mohammedanism, Parseeism, and Brahminism to identify themselves with Christian communities. Dr. Sherring, of Allahabad, said, that if the gospel conquests should advance for two hundred and fifty years as between 1851 and 1871, all India would be Christianized. Sheshadri, however, well adds that " God works according to a higher arithmetic of His own," and declares, " I have no faith to wait for two hundred years. From what I have noticed in our own country and other countries, the time may not be far distant when we shall have gone from sixty thousand converts to a hundred thousand, and from a hundred thousand to a million, and then within a short time the whole of India will be evangelized."

CHAPTER VII.

BURMAH AND THE KARENS.

URMAH, beyond the sacred Ganges, contains about three millions of people. A country with fine forest timber and a variety of vegetable riches, stores of mineral wealth and oil, gold-bearing sands, and mines of iron, lead, silver, and gold, and even rubies and sapphires, cannot be thought poor in resources.

Here, as in Hindostan, God has permitted British diplomacy and arms to establish an Anglo-Indian empire, controlling the seaboard from the mouth of the Ganges to the Malacca Strait, and unlocking this land also to the gospel, which, as no student of missions needs to be told, has here found a special arena for its triumphs.

The work among the Karens, especially, seems to bring us back to apostolic times.

When Mr. Boardman removed from Maulmain to Tavoy to plant there the germ of a Christian church, there lived in his family a middle-aged man who had been a slave, till the missionaries illustrated "redemption" by buying his freedom. When he left Maulmain he was already a convert to Christianity, and soon after reaching Tavoy was baptized. His name was Ko-Thah-byu, and he was one of the race of the Karens. His name will never be forgotten; for he was the first who in the Burmese Empire embraced Christianity, and afterwards for many years preached the gospel to his despised and oppressed countrymen with rare zeal and success. His conversion was a turning-point for the race to which he belonged, for it called the attention of the missionaries to them, and suggested that "mission among the Karens" which, in intensity of interest and measure of success, has scarcely been equalled by any other in modern times.

These Karens, or Karians, i. e. *wild men*, are a somewhat peculiar people, scattered over the forests and mountains of Burmah and Siam and parts of China; and, though more industrious and less vicious than the Burmese, are their inferiors physically and intellectually. They are looked down upon as slaves, and compelled to pay heavy taxes, to till the land, and do servile work for their oppressors. To avoid those who would kidnap and enslave them, they lead a wandering life, and live in regions comparatively remote and inaccessible.

These Karens, though they believed in a god and in a future state of rewards and punishments, were without any form of religion or priesthood or superstitious rites. They seemed divinely prepared for the gospel, and welcomed the good news with enthusiastic delight.

It is now nearly sixty years ago that Mr. Boardman, constrained by the importunate invitation of Karens in the interior, undertook to journey to the remoter villages with

Ko-Thah-byu as his interpreter. He found a *zayat*, built by the natives in anticipation of his coming, large enough to contain the whole population of the village, many of whom stayed all night for further instruction, and five of whom asked for baptism. After ten days he returned to Tavoy, convinced that this most interesting people ought to be reached by itinerant preaching and schools.

The story is too long to be told in these pages. Mr. Boardman's consecrated life closed after a few years' labor, and his tomb at Tavoy is significantly located in what was once a Buddhist grove, beneath the shadow of a ruined pagoda. But the work thus begun has grown with a rapidity seldom paralleled. In 1878 the fiftieth anniversary of the conversion of Ko-Thah-byu was kept by jubilee gatherings and the consecration of the Memorial Hall that bears his name. The Karens themselves built it for school and other mission purposes, at a cost of fifteen thousand dollars. It represented twenty thousand then living disciples converted from demon-worship, maintaining their own churches and schools, beside twenty thousand more who in the faith of Jesus have died and gone to be with Him in glory. At the dedication of this hall four veteran native Karen pastors and hundreds of others were present. The hall measures 134 feet on its south front, 131 on the east, and 104 on the west. It has a splendid audience-room, 66 by 38 feet, with a fine gallery. Along the east side is carved in Karen, "Behold the Lamb of God," etc.; and on the west, "These words . . . thou shalt teach diligently unto thy children." What a work may this hall see done in fifty years to come!

He who would realize what the gospel has done for the Karen slaves must go and stand on that "Gospel Hill," and see Ko-Thah-byu Memorial Hall confronting Shway-Mote-Tau pagoda on an opposing hill, with its shrines and fanes. Here is the double monument of what the Karens were and are. Burmah has not only taken her stand among the givers, but, in 1880, ranked third in the list of donors to the Baptist Missionary Union, — only Massachusetts and New York outranking her! Massachusetts gave $41,312.72; New York, $39,469.78, and Burmah $31,616.14! and of this amount the *Karen churches gave over $30,000!* Fifty years ago in idolatry, now an evangelizing power! And not content with this, they set about raising another $25,000 to endow a normal and industrial institute. Their liberality puts to shame the so-called benevolence of our Christians at home. We give out of our abundance; "the abundance of their joy and their deep poverty abound unto the riches of their liberality."

In the Government Administration Report for British Burmah for 1880–1881 there is a glowing tribute to the American Baptist missionaries, followed by the statement that there were then attached to their communion "four hundred and fifty-one Christian Karen parishes, most of which support their own church, parish school, and native pastor, and many of which subscribe considerable sums for missionary work." The report adds:

"Christianity continues to spread among the Karens, to the great advantage of the Commonwealth; and the Christian Karen communities are distinctly more industrious, better educated, and more law-abiding than the Burman and Karen villages around them. The Karen race and the British government owe a great debt to the American missionaries, who have, under Providence, wrought this change among the Karens of Burmah."

CHAPTER VIII.

THE OPEN DOOR IN SIAM.

IAM, or Syam, *the brown*, presents another peculiar opportunity for the entrance of the gospel. Within about two hundred thousand square miles of territory is a population estimated at eight millions. Little has been known of this romantic country, very few works having been published on Siam and the Siamese, until of late, when the attention of the civilized world has been turned that way. We are now beginning to know something of this second great river-basin of the Indo-Chinese Peninsula, with Bangkok, its capital, the " Venice of the Orient."

The vegetation is abundant, luxuriant, and marvellously beautiful; the fruits unsurpassed in variety and excellence. The animal kingdom is no less varied and interesting, including the famous so-called "white elephant," as the form associated with the appearing of Buddhas, and the transmigration of souls, far on their way toward the Buddhist heaven, *Nirvana.* In the soil lie undeveloped vast quantities of valuable mineral and metal, and precious stones. Though woman is by no means man's equal, even here, her condition is vastly superior to that of her sex generally in the East, and her ordinary treatment is affectionate and considerate. Social distinctions are numerous, and *numerical,*—five representing the lowest slave, and one hundred thousand the second king.

The sacred literature, in the Pali, is written with a stylus on long slips of palm-leaf, and the four hundred principal works embrace four thousand volumes. The secular consist of about two hundred and fifty principal works, with two thousand volumes. Of the males, from eighty to ninety per cent can read, and education is afforded gratuitously at the temples. Buddhism absolutely sways this people. Its sacred fanes, resembling the Egyptian in their type of architecture, are among the costliest and finest of the Orient. One is estimated to have cost $800,000, and contains nine hundred images of Buddha, the principal of which, in a reclining posture, is one hundred and fifty-eight feet long, inlaid with pearl and overlaid with gold. The priesthood once numbered one hundred thousand, but are much fewer now.

Protestant missions date from the days of Gutzlaff, Tomlin, and Abeel in 1828–1831, and properly from the settlement of Jones in 1833. Half a century ago all foreigners, whether missionaries or merchants, were excluded; now all Christian countries enjoy treaty-rights. No country on earth is perhaps more widely open to the gospel, and here the Presbyterian Church especially should concentrate her forces; for Divine Providence has especially given to this body of Christians this land to occupy for Him.

The American Baptists have had a mission there for over fifty years, but now they are working only among resident Chinese, from whom Dr. Dean, in 1837, organized the first church of Chinese Christians in all Asia. To the Presbyterians of America is thus left at present the entire evangelization of the native Siamese. To do this great work, that denomination has but two main stations, at Bangkok and Petchaburi; and two more among the Laos, at Chiengmai and Lakawn. Their entire force of missionaries, were they all on the ground, would number but *six men, twelve women*, and nine native preachers and teachers. In other words, twenty-seven workers in all, who, if their responsibility could be averaged, would have the care of three hundred thousand souls each!

Yet few appreciate the opportunity that Siam presents. The country feels throughout her extent the thrill of her contact with Western civilization. The telegraphic circuit embraces her and binds her to the Christian world. The postal system is extending from Bangkok to the bounds of the kingdom. Mercantile enterprise is developing the exports and introducing imports. The King is pronounced, next to the Mikado of Japan, the most "progressive sovereign in Asia." Himself an educated man and an astronomer, he favors education. More than this, he favors the missionaries, and has frequently made donations toward the mission work. The government gives practical proof of its estimate of the value of Christian missions by giving the land for a new mission station at Lakon. The King subscribes $1,000 for a hospital building. These are but the latest of a series of friendly acts, showing the attitude of the royal court toward the work of the mission.

With the death of the then reigning King in 1851 this new and liberal policy was inaugurated by the government. His successor, who reigned for seventeen years, was a cultivated gentleman and scholar, who had been taught in languages and modern science by a missionary of the American Board; and under the present reign the influence of Protestant missionaries with the government, as we have seen, has not waned. An official document, under royal sanction, testifies to their intelligence, integrity, and personal worth. It acknowledges the debt of the Siamese to them for teaching them to read and speak the English tongue, and says: "The American missionaries have always been just and upright men; have never meddled in the affairs of government nor created any difficulty with the Siamese; have lived with the Siamese just as if they belonged to the nation;" and furthermore, this document affirms the high standing of the missionaries in the respect and love of the government.

Siam was not opened by gunpowder or diplomacy, but by missionary influence, and the whole aspect of the nation and its attitude toward Christianity are gradually undergoing a change. The preaching, the teaching, the press, and the medical missions are the four conspicuous agencies which God is now using to bring Siam to Christ. With what results, a single example may show, and give a hint of the possibilities of the near future.

When this young King, now about thirty years old, patron of letters, science, and art, recently, by a sad accident, lost his wife, he sent his brother to the missionaries for a copy of the New Testament; and that elder brother gave as a reason for the request that the King had *lost faith in his own religion;* that he could find nothing in Buddhism to console him in his great grief. Buddhism is the State religion. It might cost the King his crown, or even his head, to espouse the Christian faith; but what meaning lies enfolded in the fact that this disconsolate monarch flies to the Christian's Bible for the solace in his bereavement, that his pagan creed is unable to supply! How much nearer may Siam be to becoming a Christian nation than many of us think!

It is an interesting fact that the first Zenana teaching ever attempted in the East was by missionary women, in 1851, among the thirty wives and royal sisters of the King of Siam.

CHAPTER IX.

THE WALLED KINGDOM.

THIS is the name by which China has been known for centuries. Its vast territory of over five and a half million square miles — five eighths as large as the whole continent of Africa, one tenth as large as the globe itself — has a population variously estimated at from 350,-000,000 to 500,000,000. No other country can claim artificial water communication of such extent; the Grand Canal, 650 miles long, is but the largest of four hundred which form the highways of the empire for transit and travel, and at the same time supply a system of irrigation. Within a country having a coast line of 3,350 miles, a frontier of 12,550, reaching through 38 degrees of latitude and nearly twice as many of longitude, we may well expect to find every variety of animal, mineral, and vegetable.

But the great attraction of China as a mission field lies in the people, who are called the "Oriental Yankees." They are industrious, frugal, polite, and capable; and while they have the vices of a pagan people, they rank even above the East Indians in the plane of their civilization. Proud of their antiquity, they have a history whose authentic records reach back to the age of fable. They may well boast of a civilization which is founded upon such men as Confucius, who was born 550 B. C., and whose death preceded the birth of Socrates by eleven years; and Zoroaster, or Zarathustra, who dates from seven hundred to five thousand years earlier, — men who stand in their relation to China where Moses does to the Hebrews, and Socrates to the Greeks.

Excepting steam-engines, electric telegraphs, and the most startling inventions of modern days, there are few great inventions which have not been in use in China for centuries before they were known outside the Walled Kingdom; even the mariner's compass, movable type, printing and paper, porcelain, silk, gunpowder, etc., being long familiar to this remarkable and exclusive people. They have a high type of popular education, civil service with competitive examinations, and a social structure on firmer foundations than any other empire, with one system of manners, letters, and policy. It is quite obvious that the specimens of Chinese character which commonly find their way to our shores are not fair representatives of this ancient and remarkable people.

In no country is it possible for capacity and fidelity to find recognition more than in the Celestial Empire. All public offices are open to graduates of the colleges, academies, and universities, without distinction of nationality, birth, class, or creed; and so brains and skill are the highways to public honors and official emoluments. Erudition, according to their standard, is the golden mile-stone from which all roads radiate in the administrative system.

The great wall, called by them the " Myriad Mile Wall," is the most gigantic defence ever built by man. It winds along the north frontier of China proper for fifteen hundred miles, from fifteen to thirty feet high, with towers rising forty feet, and is broad enough for six horsemen to ride abreast. It may well represent China's attitude toward Christian missions until the famous treaty of Tientsin, in 1858. On August 25 of that memorable year the Atlantic cable shot across the ocean-bed the news that this colossal Oriental empire was open not only to the commerce of the world, but to the gospel.

The pride of the Chinese in their ancient civilization and religious and ethical faiths presented a formidable barrier to evangelization. Their national isolation is partly the result of inordinate conceit. The Emperor is the Son of Heaven, sits on a dragon throne, signs decrees with a vermilion pencil; his empire is the " middle kingdom," his people the " celestials." The geography of the Chinese gave nine tenths of the globe to China, a square inch to England, and left out America altogether. The lexicon of their language dates back almost to the beginning of the Christian era, and the imperial library of eighty thousand volumes was ancient when that of Alexandria was burned. Yet their "golden age" is manifestly past, and for centuries they have halted and made no progress, ever resisting innovation. But as they begin to feel the power of contact and intercourse with enlightened nations, the petrified constitution and culture of four thousand years begins to lose its impenetrability and inflexibility. There is to be a railway from Tientsin to Pekin; the sea and the capital are to be united by a link of steel. As Carleton Coffin prophesied, years ago, the superstition about the " Earth Dragon " will be exploded when the Chinaman sees the railway ploughing through even the burial-places of his ancestors. Geomancy must die before modern civilization, and the gospel will take its place.

Notwithstanding their numerous religions; ancestral worship, with its tablets and shrines in every house; idolatry, with its patron god for every trade, and its annual cost of $180,000,000; Confucianism, Tauism, Buddhism, Mohammedanism, — though it be easier to find a god than a man, the Chinese are a nation of atheists; and with all their high civilization, a nation of gamblers, opium-eaters, rakes, and drunkards. Their very language has the taint of moral leprosy, and the walls of inns are painted with the "flowers" of obscenity.

Woman's condition is degraded and deplorable beyond words. Mandarin Ting said to the French traveller, Huc, "Women have no souls." The birth of a daughter is held to be a calamity and disgrace; the infanticide of girls is fearful in extent. In forty towns about Amoy Mr. Abeel found two fifths of all the girls were destroyed in infancy, — drowned or buried alive, — and commonly by the father. Mr. Doolittle says that probably more than half the families of Foochow have destroyed one or more female children. Those who are not killed or exposed are sold in infancy for wives or slaves. The husband may beat, starve, or sell his wife, and women are constantly driven to suicide.

It is reckoned that the Chinese Empire contains 1,700 cities, within which lie grave-yards containing in some cases 20,000,000 dead.

The language was another barrier to Chinese evangelization, that was as high as Babylon's impregnable walls. With its tones, aspirates, and idioms; with its 43,500 words in the official dictionary, 5,000 of which must form a scholar's vocabulary; with root words estimated at from 315 to 4,000, and 214 symbolic characters; with its complicated " hieroglyphs," one of which takes over fifty strokes; with its further complications from tones and inflections, so that one word uttered in ten different ways means

as many things, and words identical in sound
are diverse in form and sense; with its in-
capacity for sacred ideas and expression of
spiritual graces, so that for a half century
translators doubted what name to use for
God, — the Chinese tongue seemed Satan's
master-device to exclude the gospel. Yet
happily the "Mandarin," or written language,
throughout the empire is one, however different the spoken dialects. A Frenchman,
taking the elementary parts of the language,
reduced them to a few hundred; the Presbyterian Board helped him with $5,000 to com-
plete his alphabet and presses. In 1874 one
Chinaman made over six hundred stereotype
plates, and as long ago as 1875 there were
eight presses at Shanghai alone, scattering
Christian literature.

CHAPTER X.

PROTESTANT missions in China date back to 1807, when Robert Morrison, the "last-maker" of Morpeth, their pioneer, came to Canton. He had prepared for divinity school by studying all night and making boot-trees all day. Nominated translator to the East India Company's factory at Canton, he lived, ate, slept, and studied in the warerooms of a New York merchant. There, in native dress, with long nails and cue, praying in broken Chinese, and studying by night beside his little earthen lamp, this heroic man prepared to give China the Holy Scriptures in the native tongue. After seven years he baptized his first convert and completed the translation of the New Testament. Joined by William Milne, they two, in 1818, gave to that empire the whole Bible. Eleven years later the American Board of Commissioners for Foreign Missions sent Bridgman, Abeel, and others; and so the missionary band and their work slowly grew. Converts began to multiply; between 1853 and 1871 their number had increased more than twenty-fold. Missionaries were so highly respected that in one case an offer of $10,000 in gold was made them as an inducement to take charge of government schools.

Five years ago over thirty missionary societies were at work in the Celestial Empire, with something less than three hundred and fifty missionaries and teachers, over one hundred stations, and five hundred out-stations. The China Inland Mission, under the wonderful organizing power of J. Hudson Taylor, is calling to itself the eyes of the world just now, partly from its peculiar basis and partly from the fact that the university graduates, who were converted in connection with Mr.

Moody's labors, at Cambridge and elsewhere, have so largely been identified with it. It was organized in 1865, and upon five principles:—

1. It is unsectarian but evangelical, representing exclusively no branch of the Church, but welcoming friends and workers from all denominations.

2. It has no inflexible educational standard of qualification, insisting only on a fair measure of ability and acquisition, with good health, good sense, and consecration.

3. It is conducted as a work of faith, incurring no debt, asking no aid, fixing no salaries, but distributing funds as they are sent in.

4. It requires workers to identify themselves with the people for whom they labor, in dress, cue, etc.

5. It magnifies dependence on God, as the sole patron of the mission.

Its present staff is less than three hundred, and its income for 1884 was nearly $100,000. Rev. H. C. Du Bose prophesies that in ten years this mission will equal in numbers the other missionaries from all lands and churches, boards and societies.

Christian missions could not but suffer very serious hinderance by the course of events from 1820 to 1858. The disgraceful opium war left a lasting reproach on the name of England, and associated the name of Christian with an act worthy of the worst of barbarians. For years the British persisted in flooding the country with this Indian drug. Tao-kuang, seeing that body, mind, and morals were dying of the drug, in 1828 issued severe prohibitory laws, and destroyed the trade for a time, and ten years later made the use of opium a capital offence, and destroyed British stock to the amount of $20,000,000. Then followed a war which in 1842 wrested from the Chinese government concessions in favor of free trade in opium, but intensified the hatred of all foreigners.

The very inability of the Mantchoo dynasty to repel the Christian powers brought upon it contempt and hatred, and led to the formation of the secret triad society, which in

1850 attempted under Tien-te to overthrow the government, and after his death, under Hong-siu, not only carried on one of the most gigantic rebellions ever known, but persuaded Christians and missionaries to identify themselves with their cause, under the pretext that the rebels themselves were a sort of " Protestants."   This again made Christian powers obnoxious to the Chinese government.

Then followed a war, in 1856, in which Britain led the way, and it became the signal for a general crusade against China, in which France, the United States, and Russia afterward joined; and the final issue of this war was the Treaty of Tientsin, which reads as follows : —

"The Christian religion, as professed by Protestants and Roman Catholics, inculcates the practice of virtue, and teaches man to do as he would be done by. Persons teaching or professing it, therefore, shall alike be entitled to the protection of the Chinese authorities; nor shall any such, peaceably pursuing their calling and not offending against the laws, be persecuted or interfered with."

In that treaty the " wall " has been thrown down, and every man may "go up straight before him " and take possession. To all the provinces, with their seventeen hundred cities and innumerable villages, the missionaries may go, without hinderance or molestation, claiming in case of necessity protection and aid; and native Chinese may claim the privilege of both embracing and confessing the Christian faith. Well does Dr. Gracey say that "never before since the world began did any one document, so brief, admit at once to the possibilities of Christianity so large a portion of the human family, or roll on the Christian church so much responsibility. It admitted one third of the human race to the brotherhood of Christian nations. That door was opened not by the vermilion pencil of the Emperor, but by the decree of the Eternal." [1]

Dr. Williams, after thirty-two years in China, thinks that half a century more of Christian missions will evangelize, and even Christian-

[1] Open Doors, by J. T. Gracey, D.D., pp. 35, 36.

ize, the empire; Mr. Burlingame testifies that intelligent men there put no faith in the popular religions; and Dr. Bartlett finely adds that this "Gibraltar of pagandom may become its Waterloo."

These Oriental Yankees, once brought to Christ, will become the aggressive missionary race of the Orient. They are very enterprising, and swarm everywhere like bees: they are even now scattered through Siam and India, California, South America, and Australia, and will ultimately people Polynesia.

CHAPTER XI.

JAPAN, THE SUNRISE KINGDOM.

O the United States it was given to unlock the doors of this island empire, and in the light of subsequent developments it proves one of the most important events of modern missionary history.

Those sea-gates of the Land of the Rising Sun were bolted and barred for centuries. In the middle of the sixteenth century, following close upon Portuguese merchants, Francis Xavier, the famous apostle of the Indies, visited the Sunrise Kingdom, and conversions to the Papal Church were reported in vast numbers, even Japanese nobles and princes being among the converts. In 1582 the Catholic converts sent an embassy to Rome bearing letters and presents to the Pope in token of their allegiance to the Supreme Pontiff. Their return was the signal for new conquests over the native heart, and in two years twelve thousand more were baptized. The Portuguese merchants and missionaries had thus far been favorably received, and the success of the one was as great as that of the other. The haughty disdain with which these adventurers treated the Japanese, their lordly assumptions and arrogance, awakened distrust on the part of the natives. Portugal and Spain were at that time united, and a Spaniard, when asked by Taiko Sama how it was that his king (Philip II.) had managed to possess himself of half the world, unwisely replied, " He sends priests to win the people, he then sends troops to join the native Christians, and the conquest is easy." This answer was like a wind to fan the fires of distrust already kindled. In 1587 Taiko decreed the banishment of the missionaries; the edict was renewed by his successor in 1596, and the next year twenty-three priests were put to death in one day at Nagasaki. The Romish converts, instead of adopting conciliatory measures, defied the government and made war against the religion of the islands, destroying both fanes and idols. Persecution bared her red right arm, and in 1612 and 1614 many converts were put to death, their churches and schools laid in ruins, and their foreign faith was pronounced accursed, as treason both against the gods and the state. Even the Portuguese traders were driven out, and allowed access only to the island of Desima. Again, in 1622 a horrible massacre of native Christians revived the persecution; and when, fifteen years later, it was found that a conspiracy had been formed between the Japanese Roman Catholics and the Portuguese and Spaniards to overthrow the imperial throne and set up the Papal See upon its ruins, persecuting violence swung to its last extreme. Edicts were issued forbidding Japanese, on any pretext, to quit the country, and decreeing that *if any Christian, or even the Christian's God himself, should set foot on the islands, he should lose his head.*[1] By the close of 1639 the Portuguese were expelled, and their trade transferred to the Dutch, who, as their enemies and the enemies of Roman Catholicism, were tolerated. In 1640 the native Christians openly rebelled, seized a fort, and were only subdued by the aid of the artillery and military science of the Dutch. When their stronghold fell the thousands within its walls were indiscriminately slaughtered; and henceforth intercourse with foreigners was suspended, and even the Dutch were confined to the island of Desima.

This distrust and dislike of foreigners kept the ports of Japan shut even against vessels of commerce, until the middle of this century. In 1852, in consequence of complaints as to the treatment of American seamen who had been wrecked on the Japanese coast, the United States sent Commodore M. C. Perry

[1] The exact form of this ancient edict is as follows : —

"So long as the sun shall warm the earth, let no Christian be so bold as to come to Japan ; and let all know that the King of Spain himself, or the Christian's God, or the great God of all, if he violate this command, shall pay for it with his head."

with an expedition to demand protection for American ships and their crews and secure a treaty for purposes of trade.

In 1853, on the Lord's Day, he, with a squadron of seven ships-of-war, cast anchor in the bay of Yeddo. Spreading the American flag over the capstan of his vessel, he laid thereon an open Bible, read the One Hundredth Psalm, and then, with his Christian crew, sang from Kethe's version : —

> "All people that on earth do dwell,
>   Sing to the Lord with cheerful voice ;
> Him serve with mirth, His praise forth tell,
>   Come ye before Him and rejoice."

That first Christian psalm that ever sounded in the bay of Yeddo echoed over the quiet waters, the signal of a peaceful conquest. Without firing a gun or shedding a drop of blood, Japan's ports were thrown open to the commerce of the world and to the evangel of God. Perry delivered the letter from our President to the Emperor; and on March 31, 1854, negotiations were concluded and the treaty signed. Similar treaties followed in

September, 1854, with Britain, and subsequently with Russia and Holland.

Since then the progress of Japan toward the civilization of the Occident, and toward assimilation to Christian nations, has been absolutely without precedent or parallel. Between thirty and forty millions of people within the space of thirty-three years — the average lifetime of a generation — have changed in everything. Intellectually, socially, politically, religiously; in government, education, and religion; in individual life and family life; in trade and manners; in army and navy, finance and political economy, — they are scarcely recognizable. A young man, himself a Japanese convert, a student in Johns Hopkins University, speaking lately in Bethany Church, Philadelphia, acknowledged that there is nothing left as it was thirty years ago, "except the natural scenery," and that "the Light of Asia is fading and waning; but while it is at its sunset, the Light of the World is rising on that island empire."

The Mikado is to-day showing himself one of the most progressive sovereigns in the world, and the people are not far behind. In building ships and constructing machinery; in projecting lines of railway and telegraph; in establishing schools and universities; in culture of mind and cultivation of soil; in postal facilities and political economy; in banishing feudalism and disestablishing Buddhism; and in a hundred other radical changes and giant strides, — Japan is astonishing mankind. It is said that the newspaper is an index of civilization. Twenty-five years ago Japan had not one; now, there are over two thousand, — more than in Russia and Spain combined, or in all Asia beside.

Meanwhile, as all nations are going to Japan, Japan is going everywhere. The sea, which was her "bulwark," is now her "pathway," and at every capital of Europe are Japanese representatives. Caste distinctions are giving way to democratic ideas, and the old cumbersome alphabet to Roman characters; while new coinage, a new tax system, a new social life, are the marks of progress; and in 1881 the total of literary publications was about five thousand. In one year the total increase in the number of pupils in schools was two hundred thousand.

At the beginning of the present year (1886) the old ministry with its privy council gave place to the modern " cabinet," and the Mikado decrees the intelligent reorganizing of the whole administration. The new cabinet embraces eleven departments; Count Ito, the President and Premier, and Count Inouye, who is Minister of Foreign Affairs, and next to him in prominence, and Mr. Mori, head of the department of education, are declared to be the most progressive men in the empire. Mori officially orders the organization of the Imperial University at Tokio, in five colleges, — of law, medicine, engineering, letters, and science, — with branch institutions in four other cities. The people accept the new *régime*, and are to choose in 1890 a constituent assembly.

In all these changes Christianity is a prominent, though partly unconscious, factor. In 1873 the calendar of Christian nations displaced the pagan, and *Anno Domini* determines all dates. In 1876 the national " fifth day " gave way to the " one day in seven " as a day of rest. The ancient edict against Christians, though unrepealed, is a dead letter; absolute toleration is openly advocated by editors, orators, authors, and statesmen; and prominent leaders, as a measure of political economy and national advancement, advise the acceptance of Christianity as a state religion.

Mr. Fukuzawa, who three years ago published a book urging that Christianity be not even tolerated within the empire, recently completely changed his ground, and a series of articles from his pen appeared in the " Jiji Shimpo," urging with equal vehemence the *adoption of Christianity by the Japanese;* and this not as a religious convert, but on purely economic and political grounds, as the best thing for Japan ethically and socially.

Gracey says, " Japan is ripe for the Christian religion as no other is on the globe; and *it is possible Japan may become Christian by royal decree in a day.*" The people, hungry for the gospel, crowd even the theatres to hear the preacher, and the whole aspect of missionary work in Japan is as fascinating as a romance, while it is awful with the responsibility and reality of a present and pressing duty, which no language can sufficiently emphasize.

At the last Triennial Conference of native Christians at Tokio, forty of the native pastors and workers were present from different mission boards. What a signal mark of the rapid movement of missions in Japan, since fifteen years ago nearly every one of these converts was enveloped in the death-shades of paganism!

Only thirteen years since, the first Protestant church was formed, yet now there are a hundred and fifty, and from thirty-one of these connected with the American Board came a congratulatory letter prepared by the native Japanese pastors, and addressed to the Board at its great anniversary. Meanwhile Buddhist priests are in danger of being driven to work to avoid starvation. The popular faith in Buddhism is about dead, and instead of the vast sums formerly spent on temples, it is estimated that not more than $150,000 are now expended, and an ex-daimio sent $500 and a chandelier as a present to the mission church at Sanda at its tenth anniversary.

Yet people see only what they want to see. A lady spent eighteen months in Kobe, and opposite a chapel where there was preaching every Sunday. She reported that she had never seen *one native* enter that chapel, and that missions were accomplishing nothing for the evangelization of Japan. It was a chapel *expressly for foreign residents*, and had nothing to do with the missions, whose premises were in another part of the city.[1]

[1] Compare "Ely Volume," Introduction, p. vii, for a similar instance in Syria.

CHAPTER XII.

KOREA, THE HERMIT NATION.

KOREA, though the last of the hermit nations to be opened to the gospel, we consider next, on account of its proximity to China and Japan. It has been suddenly thrown open to evangelistic labor after a strict isolation of centuries. Its territory is partly peninsular and partly insular; the peninsula extends southward between the Yellow Sea and the Sea of Japan; it is about four hundred miles long and one hundred and fifty miles broad, and is shaped almost exactly like Italy. Numerous adjacent islands, greatly differing in size, constitute the Korean archipelago; they are chiefly of granite rock, some rising two thousand feet above sea-level. The population can-

not vary far from that of Siam in number,—
from eight million to twelve million. The
climate differs greatly in the north and
south; and the vegetable and mineral prod-
ucts compare favorably with those of other
lands.

The predominant religion is Buddhism,
though there are some followers of Confucius,
as in China, and some of a religion similar to
that of the *Shin-tu* in Japan. Indeed, Korea
seems in some respects a cross between these
two immediate neighbors.

In 1882 Korea was, by treaty, opened to
American commerce; but the key used by
God to unlock this empire to the gospel was
the medical mission. Somewhere between
the sixteenth and eighteenth centuries Romanism was carried into this country by papal converts from Japan and China. About
one hundred years ago Senghuni, a distinguished official, professed conversion and was
baptized under the name of " Peter; " the
missionaries were popular, and the more educated classes saw that even this corrupted

form of Christianity was an improvement upon paganism. The government became alarmed; the priesthood led on a persecution, and the Catholic converts recanted or fled to China, or endured torture and martyrdom. In 1835 Roman Catholic missions again found entrance into Korea by way of China and Mantchuria; and the Jesuits claimed fifteen thousand converts, even as late as 1857, after being again driven from the field.

But we are especially concerned with the late opening for Protestant missions. Japan in 1876 made the first complete treaty with her neighbor across the channel; six years later, partly through the aid of the great Chinaman, Li Hung Chang, a similar treaty was made with the United States. In 1884 the Presbyterian Board, at the solicitation of Rijutei, a Korean of rank, who was converted while representing his government in Japan, established a station at Seoul, H. N. Allen, M.D., a medical missionary in China, going there. The American resident minis-

ter, General Foote, gave him an appointment
as physician to the legation, which was at
once protection to his person and promise
for his favorable reception. Dr. Allen was
simply tolerated at first; but during a revolt in Seoul several persons of rank were
wounded, and recovered under his care; he
saved the life of the King's nephew, Min
Yong Ik. His skilful treatment, so in contrast with the methods of the native doctors
and surgeons whom he found trying to
stanch the wounds with wax, won the admiration of the Koreans. The King's nephew
declared that they believed him "sent from
heaven to cure the wounded." The gratitude
of the King for his medical services to the
royal family found expression in the encouragement given Dr. Allen to build a government hospital, which the King names *Hay
Min Lo*, House of Civilized Virtue, and
which is under the care of the Presbyterian
mission and the supervision of Dr. Allen.
The mission finds in Rijutei a true helper
who has devoted his energies to giving the

Koreans the New Testament in their own tongue. Mr. Arthington, of Leeds, gave the money to pay for printing three thousand copies of the Gospels of Luke and John; and so the last door opens for the admission of the gospel. The working force is increased by the addition of Rev. Mr. Underwood and Dr. Herron and his wife; and there is every indication that here, as in Japan, God is going to work a great change, whereat we shall all marvel. Papal missions, with all their perversions of Christian doctrine, God used to prepare the way in part for the entrance of the gospel. Japan, waking to the knowledge of God, has been a help to Korean evangelization. Fragments of evangelical truth, brought by stealth from the Sunrise Kingdom, found their way to the heart of Rijutei. Years passed by, and the crisis came. Rijutei was the means of saving the life of the Queen, and so earned favor with the King. At once he went to Japan, where he learned the way of Christ more perfectly, and so was led to undertake, like Luther, to give his own countrymen the Word of God in their own tongue. Here is another proof of God's seal on the work of missions. A few years ago we were just beginning missionary teaching in Japan; and now Japanese converts are proposing to go to Korea as evangelists!

We are in danger of forgetting that there are many indirect results which both prove the civilizing power of the gospel and prepare the way for higher triumphs of grace.

Resultant motion is the joint effect of opposite forces acting, for example, at right angles, and communicating to a given body an impulse that sends it in a direction between them, following a diagonal line. May this not illustrate the result of the opposing forces of Christianity and Paganism, acting on society in heathen countries, modifying, gradually changing, and transforming mankind, giving a new direction to thought, conscience, habits of life, even where conversion is not wrought?

Lord Lawrence said, "Christianity everywhere imparts dignity to labor, sanctity to marriage, and brotherhood to man. Where it does not convert, it checks; where it does not renew, it refines; where it does not sanctify, it subdues."

CHAPTER XIII.

THE OTTOMAN EMPIRE.

THE Ottoman Empire, before the treaty of Berlin, comprised large tracts of contiguous territory in Europe, Asia, and Africa. The possessions of the Sultan were divided into " mediate," or those whose pashas are appointed directly by the Sublime Porte, and " immediate," or those whose governors are selected by themselves but approved by the Sultan and paying tribute to him as the higher sovereign.

Dr. Kolb, twenty-five years ago, estimated the adherents of various religious faiths in European and Asiatic Turkey at somewhat over 31,500,000, of whom over one half were Mussulmans, about one third Greeks and Armenians, about one fifth Roman Catholics, and the remainder Maronites, Nestorians,

Jews, Syrians, etc. In no country, perhaps, beside do we find so great a variety of races and religions.

The predominant influence is, however, Mohammedan, as also is the State religion. Previous to 1856, a Mohammedan of Turkish birth who became a Jew or a Christian rendered himself liable to the death-penalty, as Mohammedanism is universally intolerant. But in that year a *hatti-sherif*, or *hatti-humayum*, as it is called, was secured, by which decree the Sultan abolished this penalty, and conceded to all persons within his dominions the right to embrace any religion.

Whatever may be said of the conduct of the British East India Company, and of the legitimacy of the methods by which an English empire in India was secured, there is no doubt that God has used both that company and that empire as means of preparing a level and open highway for the gospel. Turkey lay about midway between the British Isles and the East Indies, and *en route* between London and Calcutta. Turkey might at any time take the attitude of resistance and block up England's way between the home government and her Indian empire. A sultan who could lock the gates of the Golden Horn, obstruct the passage across the Isthmus of Suez to the Red Sea, blockade the ports of Syria, dispute the right of transit from the Mediterranean to the Persian Gulf, and thus compel British merchantmen to round the Cape of Good Hope to reach India, was a foe who must be made an ally. The very security of English empire in India made it a necessity that England should get and hold at least a " casting vote " in the councils of the Sublime Porte. Hence Britain kept her ablest diplomatist there, and the wars with Egypt in 1840, with Russia in 1855 at the Crimea, and with Persia the year later, as well as many measures of diplomacy and state-craft, were prompted by the necessity of protecting those East Indian possessions, and the highway that led to them. The line of communication must be kept open.

The only perfect security must be found in the abolition of the persecuting policy of the Moslem powers. When the Armenians were approached early in this century by missionary effort, the Sultan Mahmoud II. encouraged outrages on the native Protestants; and not until his army was defeated on the Plains of Nezib, and his own death followed, did the exiles dare to return.

In 1843, an Armenian who had embraced, and then renounced, Mohammedanism, was executed at Constantinople; this led the Christian governments of Europe to demand from the Sultan a pledge that no such insult to the Christian religion should be repeated. Four years later, the English ambassador secured imperial action constituting the native Protestants a community, separate and independent; and in 1856 the *hatti-sherif* with the signature of the Sultan formally announced the era of toleration.

Whatever may be said as to the enforcement of this imperial decree in those pashalics that are under the Sultan's immediate sway, it has been little more than a dead letter in more remote districts where bigoted Mussulmans have had control. Still we must not forget that it was the first grand step toward the establishment of religious freedom and the encouragement of Christian missions among thirty or forty millions of people.

Turkey, though by the treaty of Berlin her territory in Asia and Europe is reduced, still sways over one million square miles and over twenty millions of people; and by six articles in that treaty the subjects of the Turkish government are assured of civil and religious liberty. In 1878 Asiatic Turkey came under a British protectorate, and a "defensive alliance" was formed between the two nations, by which Britain pledged her help "by force of arms" when necessary, and the Sultan pledged himself to certain reforms, mainly having in view the protection of native Christians and Christian missionaries. As a matter of fact, however, a follower of "the Prophet" espouses the Christian faith only at peril of persecution, and practically it is not the Moslem population that is reached by mission effort, but mostly the adherents of the Greek, Armenian, and Nestorian churches.

And yet we must remember that even Mohammedanism, which has most stubbornly opposed all gospel advance, is not without hopeful features.

First, it is iconoclastic. From the beginning the foe of idolatry, it is in sympathy with our simple Protestant worship.

Secondly, it is monotheistic, affirming one God, and drawing a large part of its doctrines from the religion of the Old Testament.

Thirdly, God has made it, all unconsciously and unwillingly, the handmaid of the gospel. The Arabic is the sacred language of the Koran, and curiously enough the Moslem faith enjoins upon all true followers that they be able to read that sacred book, and yet forbids its translation into any other tongue. Hence whatever be a Mohammedan's native language, he aspires to read the Arabic because it is the *only* sacred dialect of his religion and of his Bible. Now, who shall doubt a providential purpose in all this?

There is no doubt that, notwithstanding all the hostility of the Mohammedan power to evangelical religion, and the antagonism of Oriental churches that have a name to live but are practically dead, the gradual transformation of the whole community jus- tifies the concentration of large missionary forces in the Ottoman Empire.

The influence of enlightened Christian governments is permeating this whole do- minion over which is unfurled the green flag of the Prophet. The Turkish courts have been a farce, scarcely equalled in history. The Code Napoléon displaces the Moslem code in moulding the administration of law. The principles of political economy are coming to be recognized and adopted as the basis of government.

Education is making rapid progress. There are graded schools, with improved text-books; and even girls are now finding an open door to the higher education; but the supply is far from equal to the demand. The sluggish intellect of the Turks is awaking, and now is the time to take possession of its aroused faculties. For years the one chief source of reading matter to that people was the Christian missionary press; by that the Word of God has been spread through the empire, and over a thousand different books and newspapers beside. There is a nominal censorship to which books and tracts are subject, and which just now there is an effort making to render more strict; but practically it has not hindered the publication and circulation of Protestant literature.

For nearly fifty years the American Board has been working to infuse new spiritual life into the Oriental churches; and now the hour seems to have come when God opens the door for direct labor among the Moslem population. Owing to the abolition of the death-penalty, persecution for religious opinion is now illegal. The law of the Koran punishes apostasy with death, but treaty obligations practically annul the Koran; and since the case of Selim Effendi in 1857 the government officials have in numerous cases been compelled to decide that converts to Christianity were not to be molested, according to the provisions of the "treaty of Paris" in 1856.

Rev. J. K. Greene, D.D., of Constantinople, says that the scandal of Oriental Christianity has largely ceased to hinder the conversion of the Turks. The introduction of a purer evangelical faith and life contrasting with the idolatrous worship and immoral practices of these nominal Christians has enabled these Turks to see that these scandalous teachings and lives are not the fruit, but the perversions, of the religion of Jesus.

Christian schools are not restricted, as the colleges at Constantinople, Beirut, Smyrna, Harpoot, and Aintab testify, with six female seminaries at other places, established by the American Board.

The "Star in the East" appeals for the immediate occupation of Constantinople by ample missionary forces, as " the capital of the Ottoman Empire, the seat of government; as the heart of the Moslem faith whose pulsations are felt in the continents of Europe, Asia, and Africa, and reach the distant Soudan and India; which rules over Palestine and affects the destinies of the Jews. Its inhabitants represent the various nationalities on whom the Holy Ghost was outpoured at Pentecost, and who anciently were comprised under the great Byzantine Empire. It is now in a condition of crisis; the tide of opportunities is more favorable now than it ever has been for evangelistic work. The races once enlightened by Chrysostom, Gregory, and Athanasius, require again the living Word, and are anxious to raise their 'fallen candlestick. The Christian workers are ready to help, and it is consequently of the utmost importance as a rallying centre."

CHAPTER XIV.

THE DARK CONTINENT.

OW strangely, yet how rapidly, God has opened the doors of the Dark Continent! Only a few years ago, when we were studying geography, the vast district in the interior was marked on our maps " unexplored." We knew little of Africa except its six thousand miles of sea-coast, and its great desert, and that narrow border of country which lay next the ocean or lined the Nile. The heroic Livingstone, entering from the south, seeking to know something of the unknown and open a path for the missionary, after forty attacks of fever died on his knees in a grass hut amid the swamps near Lake Bangweolo, early in May, 1873. His death sounded the new signal for the evangelization of Africa. Livingstonia is the first-fruits of that dying prayer for Africa. The churches of Scotland united in its foundation, and in May, 1875, the party of missionaries left Scotland, reached the mouth of the Zambesi, and put together their mission vessel, — the steam-launch transported in parts, — and in October the "Ilala" steamed into Lake Nyassa. The missionary band, with headquarters at Bandawe, began to survey the lake, erect buildings, make roads, and till the soil; to establish medical dispensaries, with competent physicians; to gather children into schools; to give the people the Scriptures and a Christian literature in their own tongue; and to preach the gospel, gather converts, organize churches, and educate a native ministry.

A stupendous work to undertake! No wonder Professor Drummond confessed his scepticism as to the results of such a scheme amid such a people. Yet he himself sat down at Dr. Laws's station with the seven men and two women who were first-fruits of that mission, and with them partook of the Lord's Supper, and saw in them the promise of Africa's regeneration.

Livingstone's death set in motion many other agencies for the evangelization of the Dark Continent, and among them all none is to be more emphasized than Livingstone's influence on Stanley. In a recent interview, this distinguished explorer said : —

"I have been in Africa for seventeen years, and I have never met a man who would kill me if I folded my hands. What has been wanted, and what I have been endeavoring to ask for the poor Africans, has been the good offices of Christians, ever since Livingstone taught me, during those four months that I was with him. In 1871 I went to him as prejudiced as the biggest atheist in London. To a reporter and correspondent, such as I, who had only to deal with wars, mass meetings, and political gatherings, sentimental matters were entirely out of my province. But there came for me a long time for reflection. I was out there away from a worldly world. I saw this solitary old man there, and asked myself, 'How on earth does he stop here? Is he cracked, or what? What is it that inspires him?' For months after we met I simply found myself listening to him, wondering at the old man carrying out all that was said in the Bible: ' Leave all things and follow me.' But little by little his sympathy for others became contagious ; my sympathy was aroused ; seeing his piety, his gentleness, his zeal, his earnestness, and how he went quietly about his business, I was converted by him, although he had not tried to do it. How sad that the good old man should have died so soon ! How joyful he would have been if he could have seen what has since happened there ! "

No sooner had Livingstone's death become known than this intrepid explorer determined to become his successor in opening up Africa to civilization. Entering at Zanzibar in 1874, in 1877 — after a thousand days — he emerged at the mouth of the Congo, and the greatest step in the exploration of equatorial Africa was thus taken. So soon as the news reached England, the next vessel that sailed for Africa bore missionaries. They began to plant stations from the Congo's mouth to the equator, as well as about the great lakes of the East; and

now all Christian denominations seem con-
centrating upon the Congo basin to carry
on with speed and vigor the work of evangelization, and fulfil the prophecy of Krapf,
that "a chain of missions" would yet be
established there between the East and the
West.

The explorations of a quarter of a century
having unveiled Africa, the work of exploration is so rapidly going on that the maps of
yesterday are obsolete to-day, and nothing
but the *outline* of the continent is as it was
twenty-five years ago. At least five great
lakes are now discovered and surveyed, —
Victoria Nyanza, Albert Nyanza, Tanganyika,
Nyassa, and Bangweolo, — which remind us
of our five great American lakes. Five great
rivers run to the four points of the compass,
— the Zambesi, Nile, Congo, Niger, and
Orange, — with many great tributaries, providing ten thousand miles of river roadway.
Victor Hugo's prediction is already true, —
that in the coming century Africa would be
the cynosure of all eyes.

Perhaps no more wonderful occurrence has been recorded since Pentecost than the Berlin Conference that, in the closing weeks of 1884, met to determine the Constitution of the Congo Free State. King Leopold of Belgium, losing his dear son, adopted Africa with her sable children as his own, out of his royal fortune giving a princely sum annually for her sake. What an event was that when, under the presidency of Prince Bismarck, fifteen nations, by their representatives, assembled to form the " International Association of the Congo"! Article VI. contains the pith of the whole Declaration: —

" All the powers exercising sovereign rights, or having influence in the said territories, undertake to watch over the preservation of the native races and the amelioration of the moral and material conditions of their existence, and to coöperate in the suppression of slavery and, above all, of the slave-trade ; they will protect and encourage, without distinction of nationality or creed, all institutions and enterprises—religious, scientific, or charitable — established· and organized for these objects, or tending to educate the natives and lead them to understand and appreciate the advantages of civilization. Christian missionaries, men of science, explorers and their escorts and collections, to be equally the object of special protection. Liberty of conscience and religious toleration are expressly guaranteed to the natives, as well as to the inhabitants and foreigners. The free and public exercise of every creed, the right to erect religious buildings, and to organize missions belonging to every creed, shall be subject to no restriction or impediment whatever."

And who are the national parties to this most remarkable compact for civil and religious freedom? Not only Protestant powers, like the United States, Great Britain, Prussia, Denmark, Norway, and Sweden, but the Greek Church, as represented by Russia; the Papal Church, as represented by Austria, Belgium, Spain, Portugal, France, and Italy; and even the Moslem power, as represented by Turkey! The grandeur of the event overwhelms us! When, in the history of the world before, have Protestant, Greek, Papal, and Moslem powers conferred and combined to assure civil and religious freedom to a new state just emerging out of obscurity and semi-barbarism into an enlightened civilization? Were Galileo now alive, he would certainly say, of this world, "*and yet it moves !*"

And what is this "Congo Free State," thus suddenly constituted a new empire of freedom? It is a rich area of one and a half million square miles, one of the richest countries of the globe, with the noble Congo and its many navigable affluents, presenting a water highway of from five to eight thousand miles, and connecting with great lakes whose shore lines would measure three thousand more; with a population of fifty million people; with marvellous variety of scenery, climate, product, fauna and flora. When, in 1877, Stanley completed his tour of Central Africa, he had been nine hundred and ninety-nine days from Zanzibar. He could now, as he says, " in forty-three days after leaving Glasgow, be housed in his own station at Stanley

Falls, and instead of running a gauntlet for his life, from the day he reached Vivi his ascent of the river would be one continued ovation."

Well may all eyes turn to Africa. God is disclosing by His providence the great mineral, metallic, and vegetable resources of the interior. The ostrich is more profitable than the South Down mutton; the elephant-tusks will supply the demand for ivory; and so, through the very avarice of men and the higher love of science, the great unknown continent is to be crossed with a net-work of railways, penetrated in every direction by travellers and explorers, settled by adventurers and far-sighted traders, and planted with Christian missions. Already steamboats sail the rivers and great lakes; roads are being built and railways constructed, and a submarine cable laid. Before this manuscript can take the printed form, changes will have taken place which make this chapter out of date!

If this is a wide door of opportunity, what

shall be said of the obligation?   In Stanley's journey of seven thousand miles from Zanzibar to Banana he saw neither a Christian disciple nor a man who had even heard the gospel message!

CHAPTER XV.

PAPAL LANDS.

OD has, in just as wonderful ways, thrown open wide the door to the dominions of the Pope, both on this continent and on the continent of Europe.

As to Europe, it is one of the wonders of the ages that changes so radical and revolutionary should have taken place. In the age succeeding the Council of Trent papal Europe meant the oldest and grandest of monarchies: the German Empire, the political and military centre; France, the intellectual and social centre; Spain and Portugal, the "centre of expansive force;" Italy, the historical and ecclesiastical centre of all. Papal Europe then represented all the old, polished languages, and held every great historical city, ancient university, and every influential centre of letters, art, and civilization, except those developed after the Reformation.

At the time of the Reformation the control of Europe was held in the firm grasp of Rome. Great moral and political revolutions have cut off England, Scotland, Holland, Denmark, Sweden, Prussia, and part of Germany and Switzerland; and even the countries that have not thrown off allegiance to the Pope have undergone great change. Papacy has lost beyond calculation or restoration, and nowhere more surely than in Italy itself. "Papal Europe" has now a different meaning. Protestantism has been and is steadily gaining in numbers, wealth, prestige, and in power, intellectually, morally, politically, and spiritually.

The *balance of power is reversed* since 1789. At the period of the Reformation Spain and Portugal and Austria were the dominant powers in Europe. Spain, that made England quake at the terrors of her "Invincible Armada," had three times, and some say six times, the population of England; now

England, after colonizing India, America, and Australia, has twice the population of Spain. During fifty years past England has gained 119 per cent; Prussia, 72; Austria, 27; France, 12; or, taking excess of births over deaths, if France be represented by 1, Austria will be represented by 3, Russia by 5; but Prussia by 6, and Britain by 8! In 1825, Protestant population was to Papal as 3 to 13, and in 1875 as 1 to 3.

Italy has undergone transformations which are incredible to one who has not witnessed them. Where two thirds of the people could not read or write, education is now compulsory. Where the very conscience of the people seemed paralyzed, and the sense of personal responsibility and accountability dead, we have seen the Church party in Rome opening numerous schools, issuing cheap literature in large quantities, establishing soup-kitchens, relieving poverty, and informing ignorance. Where the Pope swayed with an absolute sceptre, Pius IX. was a prisoner in the Vatican, bewailing the loss of temporal power; and it is obvious to the world, if not to the College of Cardinals, that the spiritual sceptre also is broken, or at least very loosely held. The Pope will never again make emperors bow as penitents before him, or torture heretics in the dungeons of the Inquisition.

The ignorance which is the mother of superstition is giving way before the intelligence that is the handmaid of faith and devotion. In fact, as to the papacy, we mark a grand crash in the whole wall which has shut out the Bible and the pure gospel from the people. It is like the falling of the ramparts of Jericho before the trumpet-blast of Joshua's hosts; and wherever the army of God faces Romanism, every man may march into the breach straight before him and take the city.

We can hardly credit it that twenty-two Protestant churches [1] and a score of Protes-

---

[1] We find this paragraph in a late paper: —

"The foundations for the twenty-second Protestant church have just been laid in the city of Rome, Italy. Most people will be surprised to know that there are so many Protestant churches in Rome. It is only fair to say,

tant schools are now found within the walls of the Eternal City; that Rome itself is open to the circulation of the Bible and the preaching of the cross; that under the shadows of St. Peter's and the Vatican Protestants may worship unmolested and carry on the work of evangelism; that the Bible-carts roll out of Madrid, and in the very Spain whose name is the historic synonym of the Inquisition the people should so clamor for the Word of God that copies cannot be printed fast enough to meet the demand; that in France, that right arm of the papal power for centuries, land of the exiled Huguenots and of awful St. Bartholomew, both French Chambers order elimination of priests and nuns from government schools within five years; and that the greatest work of popular evangelization ever known should now be in progress, and the government aid and encourage the McAll stations, as the best possible *police* to restrain and re-

however, that they are mainly intended for the foreign residents in that city, although some of them are engaged more or less in the work of proselyting from the Roman Church."

form that mercurial people whose very blood, like the Irishman's, is quicksilver.

Savonarola's dying cry was, "O Italy, I warn thee that only Christ can save thee! The time for the Holy Ghost has not come, but it will!" What if that martyr of Ferrara could have seen Italy's history from 1848 until now! Where in 1866 a Protestant preacher was expelled for preaching, twenty years later Leo XIII. says to his cardinals, "With deep regret and profound anguish we behold the impiety with which Protestants freely and with impunity propagate their heretical doctrines, and attack the most august and sacred doctrines of our holy religion,— even here at Rome, the centre of the faith and the zeal of the universal and infallible teacher of the Church!"

What we may now see, or have seen, in Italy and Spain and France, is but a type of what to a greater or less extent is true of all lands held under the nominal control of the papacy. The "twelve hundred and sixty" days of dominion seem to have expired. No man can foresee the changes that within ten years may yet take place. There are many indications that there is to be a *Reformed* Catholic Church, on a great scale, in which those who within the papal communion hold to evangelical truth shall find a refuge from companionship and complicity with error and heresy and iniquity. Rev. W. F. Bainbridge, whose "World Tour" did so much for missions, met in Asia many Catholic priests who seem to have been influenced by the accompanying evangelical missions; and there are many signs in the British provinces and in our own republic that Roman Catholicism, in close contact with Protestantism and remote from the papal centres, is being essentially modified by such contact. The future may show us a great exodus from Rome of those who "come out of her, that they be not partakers of her sins nor receive of her plagues;" nay, even a reconstructed church, that casts off the cerements of the sepulchre, and comes forth in a new life of purified faith!

CHAPTER XVI.

MEXICO, LAND OF THE AZTECS.

EXICO, our near neighbor, is larger than all of the United States east of the Mississippi, having a total area of about eight hundred thousand square miles, and a population of at least ten millions, — one fifth of whom are of pure European blood, nearly one fifth native, and the rest mixed.

The great cordillera of the Andes, which traverses South America and is depressed at the Isthmus of Panama, then divides into two great arms, — one to the east, along the Gulf, one to the west, along the Pacific, enclosing a high table-land, crossed by sierras, broadest and highest at Mexico City. This remarkable country, though in the torrid zone, has therefore its hot and cold and temperate regions, as climate depends on altitude rather than latitude; and the Spanish language is spoken by 63,690,000 people, second in importance only to the English as the vehicle of commerce and communication between man and man.

Mexico is rich in resources, its wealth mainly lying in its mines. Humboldt estimated their yield from 1521 to 1803 at $2,000,000,000, and from the time of Cortes, at six times that sum. The Spanish kings held the mines as royal property, citizens being allowed to work them by paying one fifth to the government; but all such tax is now remitted, and all the six races—whites, Indians, negroes, mestizoes, mulattoes, and zamboes — are on a footing of legal and political equality.

The history of Mexico is a fascinating romance: the *Toltecs*, from the seventh to the eleventh century, builders of great cities whose ruins still exist, true founders of Mexican civilization; the *Chichemecs*, rude and barbarous, who succeeded them; the *Aztecs*, who came in about the beginning of the thirteenth century, and whose dominion at the time of the discovery of America spanned the continent. The Aztec government was an elective monarchy, and the laws were spread before the people by hieroglyphical paintings, and in the opinion of Prescott showed high appreciation of, and profound respect for, principles of morality.

The "Halls of the Montezumas" represented Schlegel's poetic conception of "frozen music." In one palace-room three thousand guests might gather, and on the roof there was room for a tournament. The temple excelled the Kremlin of Moscow for grandeur and elaborateness.

Their religion was a compound of poetry and cruelty. They worshipped a plurality of gods, but held one supreme lord; built pyramidal temples, or *Teocallis*, principal of which is the great Pyramid at Cholula; and had altars for human victims. They believed in three separate future states: the wicked they consigned to everlasting darkness; those who died of certain diseases, to a negative, half torpid state; and the good and brave they admitted to a sunlit sphere, whence they went to animate the pure white clouds and singing-birds of paradise.

They cased with brick or stone their solid pyramidal temples, and by outer stairs ascended to the sanctuaries on the summit. Human sacrifices were adopted in the fourteenth century, and grew from twenty thousand to fifty thousand annually. The priest tore out the heart and cast it at the idol's feet, and the body was devoured at the feast.

Mexico has been cursed by Romish superstition; a corrupt and avaricious priesthood built grand cathedrals, convents, and palaces, secured exemption from taxation, and so the poor and priest-ridden people had to pay the whole cost of government as well as support the ecclesiastics. The tyranny of the Church demanded such fees that even marriage was too costly for the poor, and perhaps half of the population living as husband and wife have no *legal* relations as such.

The clergy in 1852 numbered nearly five thousand; there were fifty-eight nunneries and fifteen hundred nuns. The immense revenues formerly went to the clergy, the total amount collected in 1862 being estimated at nearly $8,000,000; and the property of the clergy was estimated at $300,000,000, or one half the whole real estate, — making a total income of $20,000,000.

The Church was divorced from the State Sept. 25, 1873. There remained no longer an established religion; marriage was made a civil contract; real estate, guarded; monastic orders received a fatal blow; and the downfall of Romanism began, though the priests denounced the new legislation and threatened excommunication.

The Bible, which in 1847 had been brought in by our armies at the point of the bayonet, became the pioneer of this new civilization. One man brought one from Toluca. The reading of that book was the means of converting himself, his whole family, and his neighbors, till without knowing it they formed among themselves a Protestant church, and from the family of that one man three Protestant preachers came!

Another, in Almacate, became the owner of a Bible, and studied it daily. When dying, the priest came to "confess" him; but he who had learned that "the blood of Jesus Christ cleanseth from all sin" had already been delivered from fear of death, and triumphantly replied, "I need no purgatory!"

The work of Protestant missionaries, though met by opposition and even persecution, finds a people prepared. At the dedication of a church in Michoacan, in Rodriguez' house, eight hundred persons gathered, coming from a distance of from fifteen to forty miles. Señor Torcada wrote from Titacuaro, "The great majority are casting away idolatry and worshipping God."

The new government is the ally of reform, and, to an extent, even of evangelization; God permitted Maximilian to lay, unconsciously, the foundation of a revolt from despotism and Romanism. Witness the conversion of monasteries and other sacred buildings to secular purposes; the overturning of religious orders, so that there is neither "monk, nun, friar, nor Jesuit." The Palace of the Inquisition is turned into a medical school, a convent into a law school, a monastery into a training school, and Catholic churches into Protestant chapels. Witness the confiscation of ecclesiastical property, and its appropriation to educational purposes; the establishment of five thousand schools; and the general trend of events in the direction of a higher, nobler, better life for Mexico.

Business enterprise is building a vast railroad and telegraph system, as a scaffolding for the church of God. Mexico is opening to trade and travel. A people, in fetters for centuries, have had the bastile of superstition demolished before their eyes, and are dazzled by the new light that is breaking upon them. But here again *delay risks everything!* Will not the Protestant church of America awake to the duty of the hour?

Into this open door of Mexico American Christians especially ought eagerly to press and push evangelizing forces. This great land is near, needy, neglected, but hopeful. If their newly found liberties are to be a permanent blessing, intelligence and industry and evangelization must displace ignorance and idleness and superstition. For four hundred years they have been victims of slavery and oppression, and, by the confession of a Catholic bishop, not fifteen per cent of the people could read or write. They rise every morning and look toward the sunrise for the second coming of Montezuma, whom they connect with the golden age of the past and of the future. What a blessing if they can be enabled to see advancing from the east, not Montezuma, but the Redeemer of the world, heralded by the Christians of this republic!

CHAPTER XVII.

WHAT has been written of Mexico may, to a great extent, be written of the entire southern half of this continent. That wind bearing southwest and that flight of paroquets that providentially diverted Columbus from the mainland of North America, at first to the Bahamas, and so, in his third voyage, to the mouth of the Orinoco; that divine interposition that swept the caravel of Amerigo Vespucci at first to Paria and afterward to Brazil, — left the continent of North America to be discovered by John Cabot and Sebastian Cabot, the vassals of the English kings, Henry VII. and Edward VI. The same hand of God which thus gave this land to England and Protestantism, permitted the southern continent to come under the sway of papal crowns. And so this vast peninsula with its fourteen States waits to be "discovered" anew by Protestant Christians and evangelized. The conditions have been strikingly similar to those of Mexico. In fact, the dominion of the Pope stamps all countries under his absolute sway with a stereotyped political, social, and moral life, so that from one we may infer the rest. We shall find, in proportion to the measure of papal control, ignorance, superstition, priestcraft, formalism, a low standard of morals, a fettered intellect, and a perverted conscience.

Missionaries to South America have found everywhere two things, — universal *spiritual destitution* and formidable *antagonism*. And yet it is plain that these priest-ridden masses are weary of their thraldom, though scarce ready for the liberty of the gospel. Especially among the men and youth there is no love for "the Church," — at the best only a lingering fear; deism is widespread, practical immorality everywhere prevalent, and no conception of a spiritual type of piety; in fact, no feature is more marked than general religious *apathy*.

The priests threaten all who dare to go to a Protestant place of worship with the ban of excommunication, and often lead the way in acts of lawless violence toward missionaries and mission property. Civil war, with the anarchy it brings, often interrupts mission work; and yet it is plain that God is "overturning" as He has seldom overturned anywhere, in preparation for His reign whose right it is.

Material progress is visible. Better dwellings, farming implements, roads, bridges, factories and mills, railroads, steam-boats, telegraphs — in fact, all the marked features of a higher civilization, are rapidly impressing themselves on this great country. The people may not love Protestantism for its spiritual religion, but they see that it is everywhere linked with civil and religious freedom, with aggressive enterprise, good government, and national prosperity; and as they look at their own condition, — no intelligence or intellectual progress, low moral standards and lower moral practices, in bondage to a jesuitical priesthood, and living the lives of slaves rather than free men, — they naturally turn to Protestantism as a help to political and national progress.

Where Protestant missions are once planted and firmly rooted, marked changes begin in the whole social life. Bibles begin to be scattered, schools established, a pure gospel preached; and instead of the atheism that springs out of the ruins of Romanism, evangelical doctrine and practice burst into bloom.

Among all the fourteen South American States, Chili takes the front rank in intelligence and enterprise, as Brazil does in territorial area.

Chili, that has been independent of Spain since 1818, and recognized as such since 1846, within twelve months expelled the papal nuncio, suppressed the attempt of the clergy to incite revolution, carried the triumph of the liberal party through both houses of Congress, enacted important reforms in the shape of laws for civil cemeteries and civil marriages, and declared in favor of final and complete separation of Church and State.

The mission work has some notable features, conspicuous among them the seminary at Santiago, which is a training school and theological seminary to prepare a native ministry. Alexander Balfour, Esq., of Liverpool, who in many ways aided the work, pays for five years the expenses of Rev. Mr. Allis, who has the seminary in charge.

Brazil, whose territory covers about half the continent of South America, issued its Declaration of Independence in 1822, and was recognized by Portugal as a free and independent State in 1825. It is the only monarchy in South America. The present Emperor, Dom Pedro, who has reigned since 1841, is a progressive sovereign. In 1866 he emancipated his own slaves; in 1871 passed a law providing for gradual abolition of all slavery in the country; and in our centennial year visited the Great Exposition in Philadelphia, made our schools, manufactories, political and educational system a study, and then visited Europe; returning to his own people to make his throne the centre of all humanizing and civilizing influences.

During his absence the Romish party used the opportunity to hinder Protestant missions; but on his return a cabinet was formed in sympathy with the advanced and liberal policy of the Emperor and the growing popular sentiment, and the mission work received a new impulse and impetus. The papal power is broken, freedom of worship established, missionaries are protected, and another door, great and effectual, is opened by God to Christian evangelism.

Though a monarchy, Brazil has a General Assembly, with senate and chamber of deputies, similar to the English Parliament or the American Congress.

The Huguenots were the pioneers in the effort to evangelize Brazil. Admiral Coligny, the heroic martyr of St. Bartholomew, as early as 1555 planned to colonize the Brazilian coast as a refuge for Huguenot exiles, and they settled on the island of Villegagnon. This colony was short-lived. The Methodist Episcopal Church, which has the honor of leading the American churches in mission work in South America, from 1836 to 1842 maintained a station at Rio de Janeiro. The Presbyterian Church has now vigorous missions in the United States of Colombia, Chili, and Brazil, with over eighty missionaries, male and female, there at work. But what are these among so many? Would that they could be multiplied as the loaves and fishes were! We have but one Protestant missionary to six hundred thousand souls in South America. God is greatly blessing the itinerating tours which, after the example of Paul, distribute the labors of these few men over a wide field, preaching the Word over extended districts, and preparing the way for the local preacher and pastor.

Now is the golden opportunity for evangelizing South America. All times of transition are crises. The old is broken up, but what the new shall be is ours, under God, to determine. God has given us convincing proofs that Protestantism is the lever to uplift these peoples to a higher plane. Prompt and vigorous occupation of the ground, earnest, consecrated evangelism,—what might they not do for South America! With Protestant schools, colleges, and seminaries; with an evangelical press to scatter the leaves of the Tree of Life; with churches gathering converts and organizing them into evangelists; with earnest Christian men to become lawyers, doctors, statesmen, judges, educators,—we might see a religious revolution from the Isthmus of Panama to the antarctic circle.

CHAPTER XVIII.

THE SUBSIDENCE OF OBSTACLES.

E have thus glanced rapidly at the opening of the doors in some of the principal fields of missionary labor, pagan, moslem, and papal. There is, however, a class of phenomena connected with modern missions, so remarkable that it should be placed conspicuously by itself. There are some barriers which have been removed so suddenly, so unexpectedly, so peculiarly, that the hand of God has been very marked in connection with them; they have subsided even before they have been encountered by the advancing mission band.

The promise that "the earth shall be full of the knowledge of the Lord, as the waters cover the sea," not only prophesies, but illustrates, the world's evangelization. The time is coming when the good news will have spread in every direction, like the omnipresent sea in its vast bed. The Church has only to be faithful to her great trust, and, like the pulsations of great tidal waves, the knowledge of the Lord shall sweep against every foreign shore, move up into every strait and bay and estuary, and " sound the roar of its surf-line " from Greenland to Australia, and from Britain to Japan and Polynesia. The gospel is destined to be all-pervasive, like the sea, the air, the light.

The sea may flood the land, either by the rising of the ocean or the sinking of the shore; and the subsidence of the land is in effect the upheaval of the sea. The disciple rejoices when he observes those mighty movements of God's grace, which, like the rapid rising of some far-reaching tidal wave, flood extensive districts of the world with the knowledge and the power of the gospel; and devout souls look and pray for the day when some such wave of revival shall sweep over the whole habitable globe. But let us not forget that, without this startling upheaval of the sea, it can make its bed on the continents, if they sink below its level. Often in the history of missions has God gone before His people, and, by the slow or sudden subsidence of opposing obstacles, prepared the way for flooding the land; and in many cases systems of false faith, or customs of formidable antiquity, that have stood like mountain barriers to keep out the gospel flood, have actually disappeared.

In fact, the more we study missions, the more we shall see that the false faiths of the world are in a state not only of decline, but of decay. An unseen work of undermining is going on, and some day we may all be startled by the general subsidence of barriers which have hitherto seemed as deep-founded and as high-reaching as the everlasting hills. A few examples may well be added both to demonstrate and illustrate this truth.

Sixty years ago, the brig "Thaddeus" was nearing the Sandwich Islands, with the first missionaries to those habitations of darkness and cruelty on board. Never was an enterprise, humanly speaking, more hopeless. Seventeen persons were going to these ten isles to evangelize them, to upheave the ocean and flood them with the knowledge of the Lord; and against coast barriers as formidable as ever the gospel encountered, — barbarism, sensuality, superstition, brutality. These people, lost to shame, went almost naked. Husbands had many wives, and wives had many husbands; and they exchanged as they would trade in any other commodity. Two thirds of all the children died in infancy by the hands of the mothers, who would choke a babe, or bury it alive in the earth-floor of the hut, to stop its crying. A nation of thieves, gamblers, drunkards, they sacrificed human beings as victims, and had neither science nor literature, however rude. Government was a farce; a taboo system made death the penalty for offences so small that they might be committed without either will or knowledge; for a common man to allow his shadow to fall upon a chief, for instance, could be atoned for only as his head lay at the feet of that chief. No words can do justice to the moral and spiritual condition of those islands. It was a question whether such a people could be saved, even by the gospel; not a few doubted whether they were worth saving. Could you expect the sea to sweep against such barriers and wash them away? It would take a thousand years!

But as the boat drew near the coast, Hopu, a native who, having found his way to this land and to Christ, was now going back, put off in a small boat for shore, and at once returning swung his hat and shouted, "*Oahu's idols are no more!*" God had gone before these pioneers. The old king was dead, the images of the gods all burned, and the first death-blow struck at the taboo system; *all this before the vessel's prow touched the beach.* The missionaries wrote in their journal: "Sing, O heavens, for the Lord hath done it!"

Ah, yes, the island system was sinking and the huge barriers subsiding; the sea need not change its level, but only move in upon the sinking land. And so in two years the missionaries began to give them a written language and literature. The first convert was Keopuolani, the king's mother. Within four years the Christian Sabbath and Ten Commandments were formally recognized by government; and so the work went on, until within fifty years the islands took their place with other Christian nations, and became themselves centres of gospel light for the darkness around. With what amazing rapidity may the sea cover the earth when He who holds the continents in His palm lets them sink below its level!

Japan also illustrates this theory of subsidence. Such a preparation as was there found for the gospel no other land ever presented to the same extent. It could not be traced to man, for Japan had been for centuries a hermit nation, shutting herself in and shutting others out. There was every reason why, according to all human expectation, the institutions and character of this exclusive people should have been found, after over two thousand five hundred years, petrified and fossilized into impenetrability and immobility. Yet God had gone before His people, and, in advance of their approach, thrown down gigantic barriers. Here was a people tired of a dual government, an oppressive feudal nobility, and a dead state religion. Revolution had paved the way for political reformation and social regeneration. A nation by temperament aggressive and progressive, divinely prepared for a new order of things, wait for a day dawn. Just at this critical, pivotal era in Japan's history, the foremost of Christian nations peaceably knocks at her doors and asks entrance. A great republic and a great monarchy, both Protestant and evangelical, approach for trade, and bring the gospel. This awakened nation finds at once a better model of government, a higher type of civilization, a loftier plane of education, and a purer form of faith; and with incredible rapidity is taking on the complexion and character of Christian nations. Was not God in this subsidence of obstacles? Was not this another example of the coming of the fulness of His time? He struck when the iron was hot, and only He could know when it was hot.

Yes, God not only chose his own way, but His own time, for opening the doors of Japan. At the very crisis of affairs, when the dual government of seven centuries was overthrown, and the Tycoon and his divided followers surrendered to the Mikado as the sole ruling power,—at this providential juncture of affairs, when the various elements of Japanese life were in a state of fusion, ready to be moulded anew, God provided a matrix in which the New Japan should take shape. Foreign commerce was knocking loudly at the long-shut gates, bringing with it Western thought, enterprise, and manners. It was not only easy, but natural, to accept the new order of things; and consequently revolutions have taken place, intellectually, socially, and relig-iously, that centuries have not wrought else-where, which astonish not only all outside observers, but the Japanese themselves.

The eyes of the world are to-day on France, beholding with astonishment the wonderful work of God there. Yet this is another instance of subsidence. France has been the right arm of papal power for centuries, and seemed, a century since, likely to develop the antichrist. How little we knew what preparations were going forward for the inflowing of the gospel tides!

In 1877, Paul Bouchard, ex-mayor of Beaune, wrote an open letter to the bishop of his diocese, renouncing Romanism and transferring his adhesion to Protestantism, on grounds of consistency and patriotism. It was not the act of a man converted to a new faith so much as disgusted with an old one. He forsook the state religion as a patriot and political economist, denouncing Roman Catholicism as the enemy of social and political progress, the ally of ignorance and superstition. His act was one echo of Gambetta's declaration that the Romish Church is the enemy of French republicanism, — "clericalism is the foe of France."

But he went beyond Gambetta, for he reproached Gambetta with atheism. Bouchard took this great step alone, and boldly wrote five tracts for the people, giving wider expression to his views.

At the same time Eugene Reveillaud, a lawyer, journalist, orator, and statesman, a college graduate and a freethinker, born and bred a Romanist, had his eyes opened to see the rottenness of Romanism, and became the champion of Protestantism, on similar grounds to those of Bouchard, and wrote a pamphlet on the "Religious Question and the Protestant Solution." Compelled to give up the papal church, he felt he could not be without a church and a religion, but had as yet no change of heart. The faithful Huguenot pastors boldly taught that Protestantism required more than a mere renunciation of Romanism; and in July, 1878, in the Protestant meeting-house at Troyes, Reveillaud arose and addressed the congregation, declaring his conversion, and manifesting a remarkable baptism of the Spirit. From

January, 1879, his tongue and pen have been enthusiastically given to the evangelization of France. He publishes a weekly paper, " Le Signal," and goes everywhere to halls, theatres, ball-rooms, and barns, to address the people, showing them the need of a new gospel of faith, repentance, and holiness.

Our generation has seen no religious movement to compare with this arising of a whole people. "There is Protestantism in the air." In Avignon, the old residence of the popes, Renouvier adds to his " Critique Philosophique " a " Critique Religieuse " to chronicle the Protestant movement; and in Belgium, Emile de Laveleye writes on the " Future of the Catholic Nations,"— a warning to all peoples of the inevitable results of Romanist supremacy!

The rapid and radical change that has come over France no one can conceive who has not been there during this quiet religious revolution. Scarce a century ago Protestants were tortured and murdered, till even Voltaire's atheism vented its invective against persecution for religious opinion, and shamed France out of her course. Then came the reaction of atheism, but no religious liberty. But under MacMahon a majority of nine ministers of the Waddington cabinet were Huguenots, though the Huguenots represented but one-twentieth of the population. November 2, 1879, Protestant worship was held at Versailles, in the palace of Louis XIV., and not far from the chamber where he died, beneath the room where Madame de Maintenon induced him to sign the Revocation of the Edict of Nantes, nearly two hundred years ago.

The news of one week would fill a journal with startling items, — people assembling in hosts everywhere, in halls, tents, and open air, listening with intense interest to denunciations of Romish priestcraft and the good news of grace; and families, fifty at a time, coming out to take their places with the Protestants. It is but three hundred years since the St. Bartholomew massacre in 1572; and already the nation is turning from Rome. The McAll Mission has developed with a rapidity unparalleled in church history, establishing new preaching stations as fast as men and money can be obtained, and finding everywhere an open door. The tides of a pure gospel that surged vainly against mountain barriers for centuries are now rushing in like a flood. But it is a case of subsidence. It is not the tide that has risen, so much as the barriers that have given way; and so France is being covered with the knowledge of the Lord.

CHAPTER XIX.

WOMAN'S WORK FOR WOMAN.

AMONG the most remarkable examples of the opening of doors and the subsidence of barriers on the one hand, and the preparation of workers on the other, we place, without hesitation, the organization of women's boards of missions and the so-called zenana work. The significance and the importance of these developments entitle them to a special and separate record.

It is now a little over fifty years ago since, under the moving, melting plea of Mr. Abeel, from China, the women of London resolved to carry the gospel to woman in the far East. This resolve was the parent of Zenana Missions. The project seemed like the wild scheme of unbalanced enthusiasts; and wise

men pronounced it impracticable and visionary.   To attempt to get access to the harems
of Turkey and the zenanas of India was like
forcing gates of steel in walls of adamant.
Yet something must be done.   The condition
of woman in Oriental empires was so destitute and desolate, so hopeless and helpless,
that it had long attracted the attention and
aroused the sympathy of the whole civilized
world.   In India alone it is estimated that
there are one hundred millions of women and
girls sunk in utter ignorance and degradation; one third of whom can neither read nor
write, one sixth of whom are widows, and of
them eighty thousand under ten years of
age.   And worst of all, these women and
girls are positively unreached by any edu-
cating, elevating, or evangelizing influence.
Words cannot convey any adequate conception of the low estate of women in almost all
the empires where the gospel has not pervaded and moulded social life.

The work was undertaken.   It is said that
the needle of a missionary's wife was the

simple instrument God used to give access to Oriental zenanas. A piece of embroidery, wrought by her deft fingers, found its way to the secluded inmates of a zenana; if a woman could do such work as that, other women could learn under her instruction; and so, with the cordial consent of the husband, this Christian woman was welcomed to the inside of his home, and as she taught his wives the art of embroidery, she was working the " scarlet thread," dyed in the blood of the Lamb, into the more delicate fabric of their hearts and lives.

And now these barriers are no more; the gates of steel are unlocked, and Christian women enter almost without restraint the homes of Turkey, India, and China. The girls are gathering into Christian schools; the increase in the number of female pupils is so rapid that in ten years it has doubled, and is likely to multiply far more rapidly in the near future. Two years ago one hundred and sixty lady missionaries had been enrolled in the work of that London Mission, and more have been added since; pupils in their zenanas numbered thousands, and in their day schools tens of thousands. Bible-women not only enter the richest homes with a welcome, but enlightened Hindus actually clamor for the education of their wives and daughters. The Church of England Society alone had, in 1883, under visitation eighteen hundred zenanas with four thousand pupils; and both the visitors and the schools are constantly increasing in numbers and influence. A "new world" of work is thus "discovered."

Leupolt remarks: —

"If any one had hinted twenty-five years since that not only should we have free access to the natives in their houses in India, but that in cities like Benares, Lucknow, Agra, Delhi, Amritsir, and Lahore, zenanas would be open, and European ladies with their native assistants admitted to teach the Word of God in them, I would have replied, 'All things are possible to God, but I do not expect such a glorious event in my day.' But what has God wrought? More than we asked or thought, expected or prayed for. His name be praised! To more than twelve hundred seraglios the agents of the Female Normal School and Instruction Society have access."

Some two years ago the Indian Education Commission reported to the government that the most successful efforts yet made to educate women after leaving school had been conducted by missionaries; that in every province of India Christian ladies had devoted themselves to teaching in the homes of native families; and recommended that grants for zenana teaching be recognized as a proper charge on public funds, etc. And it is not a year since a Mohammedan paper of Lahore urged the propagators of Islam to make effort for the instruction of women in the zenanas, alleging that the representatives of Christian women were making such inroads upon the homes of India that, unless a counter effort were made, the very foundations of Islam would be gradually destroyed.

Shaftesbury, at the jubilee meeting of the Society for Promoting Female Education in the East, said: "The time is at hand when you will see the great dimensions of the work you are now doing. Not only in India, but throughout the East, great changes are in the future." His prophecy is even now being fulfilled. This society has missions not only in India and Ceylon, but in Japan, Africa, Persia, etc. "If these women," says an intelligent Hindu, "reach the hearts of the women of our country, they will soon get at the heads of the men." The far-reaching influence of this zenana movement may be seen in one representative instance. The young queen, who came to the throne at the crisis in Madagascar, was a pupil of Miss Bliss, at the girls' central school at the capital of the island.

While God thus opened the door of access to gentile women, He moved Christian women to organize for their greatest crusade. This growth of women's boards of missions constitutes an epoch in history.

So far as we can learn, the Woman's Union Missionary Society, organized in New York in 1860 or 1861, under the leadership of the lamented Mrs. T. C. Doremus, and with the "Missionary Link" as its organ and periodical, is the pioneer in this country. This undenominational society led the way, and was the parent of the various denominational boards now found in connection with all the great Christian bodies. The one origin of all these societies was the inaccessibility of heathen women to male missionaries; and their aim was to engage the co-operation of women with existing foreign missionary boards in sending out and supporting unmarried female missionaries and teachers to heathen women.

The rallying cry first heard in London, and then so nobly echoed in New York, soon began to be repeated and emphasized in connection with the Christian women of the different Christian denominations. Early in 1868 the New England Women's Foreign Missionary Society was formed in Boston, with Mrs. Albert Bowker, president, and Mrs. Homer Bartlett, treasurer. The American Board had in 1867 sent into the field ten single women, appropriating to this object

$25,000. The women generally felt that in such enlarged efforts in behalf of their sex they should be both prompters and helpers. Woman owes to Christianity what she is, not only as a disciple, but as woman domestically and socially. Woman naturally sympathizes with her own sex, and appreciates the degradation or elevation of womankind. Not only is woman accessible only to woman in the social system of most pagan peoples, but she needs the practical illustration of what the gospel has done for woman as seen in the Christian woman herself. Such were some of the considerations which lay at the foundation of this uprising of women in Christian lands in behalf of women the world over.

Moreover, in all education woman is God's ordained pioneer. As wife, mother, sister, daughter, she sways the sceptre in the home; man may be the head, but she is the heart, of the family. The plastic clay is in her hands: she sits at the potter's wheel; and if vessels are moulded into fitness for the Master's use, a sanctified hand must preside at the wheel, where character and destiny take shape. To organize women, distinctively, would quicken interest in the spiritual welfare of their own sex, and secure larger means for the support of women as missionaries and teachers; connection with existing boards would secure the benefits of their experience and knowledge without needless trouble and expense. Christian women, thus organized, gave their energies to diffuse intelligence and increase interest as to foreign missions, and to gather offerings. In addition to existing channels, they established direct correspondence with female missionaries, and held monthly meetings to hear new intelligence and pray for the anointing of the " spirit of missions."

The collections of the first month enabled this New England society to assume support of a missionary about to leave for South Africa. In March a circular was issued, addressed to Christian women, — a model of beauty, brevity, pathos, and power. It refers to the degradation and wretchedness of

women in heathen and Mohammedan countries; to the new doors open to labor among
them; to the special fitness of woman for
this work; and to the noble service of our
women in the war for the Union, which suggests, in woman's work for woman, a more
glorious field for her in the conflict of the
ages. This circular also urges the formation
of auxiliary societies.

The first quarterly meeting was largely
attended. Letters were read from three women, all about to be living links between the
society and the pagan world; namely, Miss
Edwards, bound for the Zulu Mission, and
Miss Andrews and Miss Parmelee, bound
for Turkey. These were first-fruits, — blessing the work of the first quarter. Other
letters were read from women already in the
field, and one from the pen of Mrs. Champion, thirty-one years before, herself a pioneer
to South Africa. This society also undertook to maintain, as Bible-readers, ten native
women.

June 1st brought another meeting at the

Old South Church, and showed how fast and firm were the roots of the organization in the hearts of Christian women, and how full its flowering stalk was of the opening blooms that promised growing service. Mrs. Cyrus Stone, long since by illness driven from the Mahratta Mission, too weak to stand, sat and pleaded for the women whose low level she so well knew, declaring that if she had a thousand lives she would give them all to lift her sex to a higher plane. Mrs. Wheeler, of Harpoot, appealed to mothers to give their children, and to maidens to give themselves, to the work; contrasting the extravagant indulgence of Christian women with the self-denials of native converts, instancing a man and his wife who sold their only bed and slept on a mud floor, living for three days upon ten cents, that they might give to the Lord!

What was at first a local organization, aspiring to no broader territory than New England, like the banyan tree, bending down its branches to take root on every side, became now the parent of auxiliary organizations. And so, October 8th, in connection with the meeting of the American Board at Norwich, Conn., the New England Women's Foreign Missionary Society, with tears of joy, was christened the "Women's Board of Missions."

Here we reach a new epoch. On Oct. 27, 1868, many ladies met in the Second Presbyterian Church, Chicago, to form a similar society for the West. The States of the interior were largely represented, and more than fifty letters were read from those who could not attend. Thus, about ten months after the formation of that New England society, there sprang into life the Women's Board of Missions for the Interior.

The Women's Board of the East held its first annual meeting in Boston, January, 1869, over six hundred ladies being present, in spite of stormy weather. Rev. Drs. Clark, Washburn, Webb, and Kirk spoke of the vast amount of ability in women, needing and craving a fit field for work.

As early as February, 1869, the Women's Board of the Interior undertook the support of Miss Tyler, of Madura Mission, and of Miss Dean, of Oroomiah, Persia, and in March began to publish its quarterly, "Life and Light for Heathen Women." In May, a third missionary, — Miss Porter, of Pekin, — besides several Bible-readers, were taken under care; and in August two more, — Miss Pollock and Miss Beach; and twenty-six auxiliaries were reported. During its first year, up to Nov. 4, 1869, $4,096.77 were gathered.

At the second annual meeting of the Board of the East, the total receipts reported were over $14,000; it had thirty-two missionaries and Bible-readers, and had appropriated $3,000 for a home for single women at work at Constantinople.

To complete this sketch, it ought to be added that women's missionary societies have now become so numerous that Rev. R. G. Wilder gives a list of *twenty-two* women's boards, representing twelve denominations, and an aggregate of receipts for 1884 of nearly one million dollars. These twenty-two boards represent hundreds of auxiliary societies and bands in almost every considerable church of the land.

It ought also to be added that the steady and rapid growth of the contributions of these women's boards shows the effect of thorough system and of "organizing the littles." The contributions of the Presbyterian Women's Board, for example, as reported to the Assembly in 1871, were $7,000; in 1872, $27,000; in 1873, $64,000; in 1874, $87,000; in 1875, $96,000; in 1876, $115,000; in 1877 and 1878, $124,000; in 1879, $136,000; in 1880, $176,000; in 1881, $170,000; in 1882, $178,000; in 1883, $193,000; in 1884, $204,000; and in 1885 and 1886, $224,000. Here is an increase of thirty-two fold — from $7,000 to $224,000 — in fifteen years; and, except in three cases, — 1878, 1881, and 1886, — the amount reported is an advance on the year previous!

Chalmers used to say that in all benevolent

work one woman is worth just seven and a half men. Surely "this is the finger of God," when Christian women are organized in such a crusade to redeem their sex in pagan and Mohammedan lands from domestic and spiritual thraldom!

CHAPTER XX.

THE PREPARATION OF THE CHURCH.

HE same Divine Providence which thus opened doors, made barriers to subside, and prepared the field for the sower, educated the Church for the mission work. Though the pious and prayerful student of history may now trace the moving pillar far back into the centuries, the eyes of disciples generally were then holden that they saw it not. The rising of the morning-star of the Reformation was the signal for an unconscious preparation of God's church for the world-wide preaching of the Word. That double reformation in philosophy and religion laid the basis for purer and more primitive faith and life, gave the Bible to the people in their own tongue, made the line fainter between clergy and laity, and by striking a blow at priestcraft revived both evangelical piety and evangelistic activity. Eyes long blinded to God's true nature and man's real need began dimly to see that the race was lost, and could be saved only by the gospel, through the Church.

Step by step proceeded the divine preparation for the modern era of missions. That triad of inventions — the mariner's compass, printing-press, and steam as a motor — made all nations, neighbors, and gave winged sandals to the herald of the cross, while it multiplied and scattered the leaves of the Word of Life. Still the Church as a body seemed not only blind and deaf, but dead to all sense either of debt or love to a dying world. The proposal of missions to the heathen met, a century ago, with cold indifference, if not with sneers of ridicule; and the missionary advance of the century, of which we often speak with boasting, as though it were the glory of the Church, is simply due to the wonder-working power of God. Few persons really appreciate how necessary it was that the Church itself should first be converted to an interest in missions.

Since Luther nailed up his theses, there has been no historic hour so dark as the first half of the eighteenth century. Even England was, as Isaac Taylor said, in "virtual heathenism," with a lascivious literature, an infidel society, a worldly church, and a deistic theology. Blackstone heard every clergyman of note in London, but there was not one discourse that had more Christianity in it than the orations of Cicero, or showed whether the preacher was a disciple of Confucius, Mahomet, or Christ. In America, Samuel Blair declared that "religion lay a-dying." In France, Voltaire, Rousseau, and Madame de Pompadour led society; and in Germany, Frederick the Great made his court the Olympus of infidels.

While Collins and Tindal were denouncing Christianity as priestcraft, Whiston was calling Bible miracles grand impositions, and Woolston treating them as allegories; while

Clarke and Priestley openly taught the heresies of Arius and Socinus, and even morality was trampled under foot, — what missionary activity could there be? To diffuse such " Christianity " would be disaster; but such a type of "piety" had no diffusive tendency or power; if it had any .divine fire left, it could not spare a coal, or even a spark, to light a blaze elsewhere.

The only hope of missions lay in a revival of religion, wide-spread, deep-reaching; and that is what God gave to His church through a wonderful constellation of evangelists. Whitefield, the Wesleys, Grimshaw, Romaine, Rowlands, Berridge, Venn, Walker of Truro, Hervey, Toplady, Fletcher, — are named by Bishop Ryle as the twelve apostles of that new Reformation which, between 1735 and 1785, woke not only England but the Protestant world from the awful sleep of irreligion and infidelity. The Church was so nearly apostate that the efforts to revive her dying life were at first met with resistance. Whitefield found Scotch ministers opposing him by set days of fasting and prayer, as though he were the Antichrist; and it was the shutting of church doors against himself and Wesley that drove them to that open-air preaching which proved the great stride of the century toward the reaching of the masses.

But the Spirit of God was breathing on the dry bones. The fires, slowly kindled at first, burned brighter and hotter, caught here and there, spread far and wide, till even America, across the sea, was aflame within fifty years from Whitefield's first sermon at Gloucester. All Protestant Christendom thrilled with a re-vived evangelical faith; and, as evangelistic zeal is sure always to follow, out of these new pentecostal outpourings came the flaming tongues of witness. From the silver trum-pets pealed forth a summons to prayer for the effusion of the Spirit upon all disciples, and upon the whole habitable earth. Praying-bands responded to the trumpet-peal in all parts of Britain, and from American shores came, in 1747, the answering echo of Jona-than Edwards's " bugle-call to concerted prayer." The tidal wave of revival rose to a higher flood-mark and moved with greater force under the Haldanes, Andrew Fuller, Sutcliffe, Rowland Hill, and others.

In 1784 the Northamptonshire Association made the first Monday of each month a "monthly concert of prayer" for the world's evangelization. The revived Church, after this awful period of drought, began to pray for a great rain, and a cloud like a man's hand appeared on the horizon; and within eight years that first Foreign Missionary Society was formed in England which, in 1793, sent to India, William Carey, the heroic man who, within the thirty years following, secured the translation of the Scriptures into forty tongues, and the circulation of two hundred thousand copies. Thus the revival of evangelical faith and of concerted prayer are the two pillars on which rests the arch of modern missions.

That little cloud has grown till the whole heaven is overspread, and there is a sound of abundance of rain. During less than one hundred years the number of translations of the Word has increased fivefold, — from fifty to two hundred and fifty; of Protestant missionary societies, fourteen-fold, — from seven to one hundred; of male missionaries, eighteen-fold, — from one hundred and seventy to three thousand; of contributions, forty-fold, — from two hundred and fifty thousand to ten million of dollars; of converts, fifty-fold, — from fifty thousand to two and a half million; of mission schools, two hundred-fold, — from seventy to upwards of fourteen thousand.[1]

More remarkable still is it how God has turned the whole tide of thought in the Church since William Carey first offered to go and meet the giant Anakim of heathenism. The wave was then at its lowest ebb. Dr. Ryland could then bid Carey "sit down," and leave God to care for a lost world; and Sydney Smith could sneer at the pious shoemaker of Paulerspury, and characterize his schemes as " the dreams of a dreamer who

---

[1] These are given only as approximate figures.

dreams that he has been dreaming." A little later, the Scottish General Assembly pronounced the idea of universal missions "fanatical and absurd, dangerous and revolutionary," and provoked old John Erskine to open the Bible battery and pour into them hot shot and shell. Still later, the missionary pioneers of America timidly ventured to ask the General Association of the old Bay State whether the zeal that God had kindled in their hearts to follow Carey's footsteps was "visionary and impracticable;" and Benjamin W. Crowninshield objected, on the floor of the Senate of Massachusetts, to the proposed charter of the American Board of Commissioners for Foreign Missions, on the ground that it "would export religion, whereas there was none to spare among ourselves," not knowing that "religion is a commodity of which the more we export the more we have remaining."

And now, from that low ebb of less than a century ago, the tide has risen to a flood-mark never before reached, and is still rapidly rising. That same England that then sneered at Carey is to-day prouder of him than Macedon was of Alexander, Athens, of Pericles, or Rome, of Cicero. London lifts to its lofty pedestal in the world's metropolis, the statue of Livingstone, as a perpetual incentive and inspiration to Christian colonies to push into the heart of the Dark Continent. The Scotch Assembly now stands in the vanguard of missions, and reverences Duff almost as much as Paul; and American churches urge their columns against the ranks of pagan and papal hosts, and erect missionary lectureships in the foremost of our theological schools, to train young men to imitate the devotion of Judson and Brainerd, Martyn and Taylor.

CHAPTER XXI.

THE WHITE HARVEST FIELDS.

EFORE we pass to consider the " gracious signs," it may be well for us to sweep, as in one comprehensive glance, over the wide fields made ready for the sower, and in many cases for the sickle, by the providence of God.

We have seen how, at the outset of the modern missionary campaign, the foes of the kingdom stood as in one compact phalanx, —Herod and Pilate made friends together in opposing Christ; Oriental empires forbidding approach; Oriental religions denouncing apostasy as a capital crime; and Oriental churches, behind the empty shell of a dead formalism, hiding a hatred of evangelical faith, fully as malignant and intolerant. We have seen God making a highway for His chariot through the iron gates of heathen hostility and Christian apathy, and joining the centres of Christendom and Pagandom.

While God permitted Protestant England to plant an empire toward the sunrise, the Pilgrims were driven to these shores to sow the seeds of a Christian republic beside the setting sun. Thus Britain was unconsciously reaching out eastward and westward to lay the foundations for a world's evangelization. Then the providence of God, by the issue of conflicts in America and India, settled the question that in both hemispheres the cross, and not the crescent nor crucifix, was to be dominant.

By the middle of the eighteenth century, Asia and America, respectively, were held by the foremost Protestant powers of the world : England having a firm foothold in the critical centre of Oriental paganism, and controlling the highway to the Indies; America preparing not only to evangelize this continent, but to move westward and carry the gospel to Polynesia and across the Pacific.

Truly God's hand is in all this history. Had England not held that highway to the East, the destinies of Europe and Asia might have been changed; Turkey divided between Russia and France, if not devoured by Russia; the Greek and Roman churches crossing the mountains and swaying all Asia. He, who makes the wrath of man to praise Him, uses English power and policy to check pope, czar, and sultan; to shield converts from persecution, whether by Armenians, Nestorians, Moslems, or Brahmins; and to drive an entering wedge into the heart of Asia, to cleave in twain gnarled and knotted trunks of Oriental pagan empires.

Meanwhile, the seed sown at Plymouth develops a mighty evangelizing power, which in course of two centuries moves across the continent, and, as though there were no more sea, advances toward the eastern coasts of Asia. God has provided a counter-force, moving from the opposite direction, to meet England and oppose her cleaving wedge, as anvil opposes hammer, with the resistance not of antagonism but of co-operation. Another irrepressible conflict has come. Commerce insists, in the name of a common human brotherhood, that there shall be an open highway around the globe, and knocks loudly at the gates of exclusive Eastern empires, until they are unbarred. Then, where commerce, arms, and diplomacy open the way, the gospel quietly enters and takes possession.

Let the glory be not unto man, but unto God. The nations were building wiser than they knew in constructing this level highway for trade and travel. Back of all was the God of nations with titanic blows cleaving a way for His gospel from the gates of the Golden Horn to the Chinese Sea through the continent of Asia.

This same God who thus prepared the way for His people's advance, quickened their dull consciences and sluggish pulses to move along the lines He had indicated. When the Church, immersed in selfishness, carnality, and scepticism, is heedless both of Christian duty and human destitution, He sends a succession of evangelists, like the minor prophets of the days of Jewish apostasy, to revive primitive faith and life. He imparts a spirit of prayer, uniting devout souls in earnest supplication. He leads a few heroic disciples to dare the assault on pagan strongholds, and moves the Church to organize missionary boards to sustain and strengthen these workers and warriors. The whole plan bears, in the very unity and consistency of its parts, the marks of one providential purpose.

In view of such manifest moving of God's providence in missions, is it strange that the missionary worker feels inspired and encouraged? He moves under the very shadow of the august divine presence; he feels encompassed with God; the angel of His presence goes before him. No barriers are insurmountable, no foes formidable. Seas dry up, mountains melt to plains, the children of Amalek are routed and the giant sons of Anak repulsed, and the walls of Satan's strongholds tumble before a blow is struck.

Armies of aliens may encompass the humble herald of Christ, but his eyes are opened to see the invisible hosts of God encamping round about him to deliver him. Difficulties do not dismay his heroic soul; for he knows God is with him, and that with God nothing is impossible. He is not restrained to save by many or by few; the silver and the gold are His. He turneth the heart of man, and even of kings, whithersoever He will; and He can work so rapidly that with Him one day is as a thousand years.

The only adequate impulse or inspiration to the work of missions must be found, not on the human, but on the divine, side of the work. God's mind is in the plan; God's hand is in the execution of it. Barriers there may even yet be, insurmountable by human power; ignorance, bigotry, and superstition may wage a desperate war against the gospel, and the fight may only be the more determined as we come to close quarters. Nay, the Church may cry "retrench!" while the Lord says "advance!" may withhold men and money in her selfish avarice and world-liness; but to preach the gospel to every creature is to obey our ascended Lord, and to move on to an assured and ultimate victory.

Whichever way we turn our eyes to scan the harvest field, the signs of the times betoken the immediate duty of putting in the sickle. There are sure signs of a day-dawn. We have passed the dull gray that is the first advance herald of the morning, and even the purple and crimson tints that tell of the glory hastening on; the east shows something more than dark clouds edged with gold, — the Sun of righteousness is rising on the world! Christlieb, completing his survey, breaks forth in rapture: " Yes, the present is, thank God, the century of missions, such as has never been. In it the age of world-wide missions has begun. More than all the generations on whose dust we tread can we to-day take up the Psalm, 'All the ends of the earth have seen the salvation of our God!' Let us take to ourselves the great consolation that to-day, as never before, the work is advancing. The long and laborious process of undermining the chief strongholds of heathenism will one day be followed by a great crash."

The final triumph of the gospel is as sure as the promises of God. But we are to use prophecy, not as a sedative and narcotic, but as a tonic and stimulant. Duty is ours, results are God's. We are not responsible for conversion, but we are for contact. We are to go everywhere and preach the gospel. All are to go, and to go to all. We are to bear our witness among all nations, and leave our God to bear His witness in confirmation of our own. We are to strike for the strategic centres, the three great empires that sway the East, — Turkey, Hindostan, and China, — to guide Japan in her new awakening, and the Congo State in its new incorporation among the free peoples of the civilized world.

Fearful will be the responsibility of even hesitation, where delay may imply disaster which even centuries cannot repair. Let us promptly follow the Pillar.

CHAPTER XXII.

THE GRACIOUS SIGNS.

THE promise of supernatural signs, which was joined to our Lord's last command, was sealed, in the early history of the Church, by actual fulfilment; and disciples were thus emboldened, even in the midst of threatenings, to preach the Word. Because those signs ceased in fulness and frequency, it has been assumed that they were meant to serve a certain definite purpose through a limited period. The Scriptures assign no such limits, and the notion of such limitation was an after-thought, and an apology for their cessation.

It is to be feared that the disappearance of those early signs had some connection with the decline of primitive piety. If our Lord designed, in some supernatural form, to set His seal and sanction upon the faithful and universal preaching of the gospel, it is still plain that, when the Church lost her separate character and her pure faith and her burning zeal, and became pervaded by the spirit of the age, the conditions no more existed which were essential to the continued displays of His peculiar presence and power. It may be said that marked divine interpositions are no longer necessary, since the gospel has received its sufficient attestation. But we notice that primitive saints besought God to grant them boldness in preaching His word, by stretching forth His hand to heal, and doing signs and wonders in the name of Jesus; and seem to have regarded such interpositions as needful to such boldness.

Was there ever a day when worldliness and wickedness, materialism and naturalism, scepticism and atheism, made constant and convincing proofs of the supernatural more needful to give boldness to those who preach the Word? It is a fact that supernatural signs have always abounded, and still abound, in proportion to the measure of the response we yield to the command, "Go ye into all the world and preach the gospel to every creature."

The presence of God, by His providence, in missionary history, is not more marked than the power of His grace, in the mighty results whose only sufficient and efficient cause is the Divine Spirit. Such grace furnishes, and becomes, God's "everlasting sign." "Instead of the thorn comes up the fig-tree, and instead of the brier, the myrtle-tree;" in other words, there is a divine displacement of noxious, offensive, and hurtful growths by the fragrant, beautiful, fruitful plants of godliness and trees of righteousness; and this constitutes the standing, perpetual miracle of the ages. This is God's "everlasting sign which shall not be cut off." Other signs may fail: the deaf may no more be made to hear, the blind to see, the lame to leap, or the dumb to sing; but a greater marvel continually proves that God is Himself tilling the soil of the human heart and of human society, for the plants of heaven begin to grow, thrive, bloom, and even unbelievers are compelled to confess, "ye are God's husbandry."

These gracious signs of God's presence and power may be traced in three prominent directions: first, *in the transformation of personal character, and even entire communities*, by the gospel; secondly, in *the consecration of the laborers* themselves to a life of heroic sacrifice; and, thirdly, in the *reflex influence of missions upon the church life*, lifting it to a higher plane of unselfish giving and aggressive effort. This threefold effect, wrought on so large a scale and in so short a time, argues a final cause that is nothing short of God Himself, and it is the more indisputable from the fact that such changes have been wrought against all the hostile forces of the natural heart.

There is no plea which can be urged in behalf of missions that silences all objections so promptly, stirs the soul of a believer so profoundly, or kindles a holy enthusiasm so rapidly, as the overwhelming argument and appeal found in the triumphs of God's grace in heathen lands. If Christ has fulfilled his promise, "Lo, I am with you alway," in the interpositions of Providence, even more wondrously and gloriously has He fulfilled it in the transformations of grace. These abundantly justify the emphatic declaration already made, that, in exact proportion to the measure of our fidelity in bearing this gospel message to all men, is the measure of God's direct sanction of our work, "bearing witness both with signs and wonders, and with divers miracles and gifts of the Holy Ghost, according to His own will."

These "gracious signs" are so closely linked with the "providential signals," that already in considering the one we have been compelled largely to exhibit the other. For example, in tracing the opening of the doors in India, Burmah, Siam, China, Japan, Korea, Africa, and papal lands, we have seen Divine Providence and grace working together. Those inner walls of superstition, ignorance, prejudice, idolatry, sensuality, brutality, could never have been thrown down by mere force; they were like walls of ice, that could only be melted away. And so God simply *shone*, as only He can shine. The Sun of Righteousness exerted His power: there came supernatural light and love and life all mysteriously conveyed in one ray, before which Brahmin and Karen, Siamese and Japanese, pagan and papist, were alike made new men in Christ Jesus.

There are, however, examples of the supernatural power of God's grace, furnished in the history of modern missions, that ought to be placed by themselves, lifted into prominence, set conspicuously in the framework of our argument. They are the golden pages in the annals of missions, that shine with the inapproachable glory. We not only see the fig-tree and myrtle springing up from the same soil which bore only the thorn and the brier, but we see the twigs and leaves glowing with a celestial radiance, aflame with the same glory that made the bush burn in the desert of Horeb. This it is which makes every mission field holy ground, and inspires every true missionary with a holy passion for the work which brings such displays of grace.

In confirmation of this, we take, quite at random, a few examples of individuals, and then of communities, where God has wrought these wonders of gracious transformation. Considered singly, they present a proof of the power of God beyond the possibility of explanation by the sceptic or infidel; nay, beyond the philosophy of those who believe in the omnipotence of mere culture and civilization. Considered together, they furnish overwhelming evidence of the fact that the gospel is still both the power of God and the wisdom of God unto salvation, able to reach both the highest and the lowest type of man.

Mrs. Rhea has said that it would be a blessed thing to look at Christ through the eyes of Moses the friend of God, or David the Messianic psalmist, or Isaiah the Messianic prophet, or John the beloved disciple, or Paul the chosen vessel; but that she would rather see Jesus through the eyes of a converted pagan woman, than through those of prophet or apostle. And her words are not hard to understand. For to none of the goodly fellowship of the prophets, or the holy company of the apostles, could He appear so wondrously beautiful as to her whom, by His love and grace, He had lifted out of the horrible pit and miry clay of association with soulless cattle and beasts of burden! Woman in pagan lands has for thousands of years been unreached by any uplifting power. Even Greece, at the summit of culture and refinement, could offer her education only as the badge of a courtesan. But as soon as the religion of Jesus reached her, she found that she had a soul, and her intellectual, moral, and social condition began at once to feel the elevating power of the gospel; and in proportion as that gospel reaches, touches, moves, and moulds woman, does she become what God meant her to be, the last and best of His creation, the companion, counsellor, partner of man.

In referring thus emphatically to the work done by the gospel of Christ in and for woman, we take her only as the type of humanity in its lowest depths of destitution and degradation. However low sin and superstition have sunk man in pagan lands, woman is always found one grade lower, for she is under man's feet. The ruin is yet more absolute and awful in her case than in his. The power, that can reach and raise the lowest, can reach and raise whatever lies above it; and no better proofs are needed of what the Christian religion can do, than are found in what it has done and is doing. Nowhere can mankind, and especially womankind, be found in lower depths of mental, moral, and social degradation than they were in Australia, Polynesia, and such lands of the death-shade, whose savages were scarce one grade higher than the brutes they hunted and killed. The Papuan, Maori, and Malagasy seemed lost both to God and to humanity, —

coins whose original image and superscription were worn off; yet they were restored to humanity and to God, to be worn as precious, burnished pieces of silver on the necklace of the Bride of Christ.

CHAPTER XXIII.

THE TRANSFORMATIONS OF GRACE.

T is one of the mysterious sayings of prophecy, that in the golden age that is coming, even the wolf, bear, leopard, and lion are to be led by a little child. Already we have foretastes of the fulfilment of this prediction. That little child born in Bethlehem, who, in all His manly, godly growth in wisdom and stature and in favor with God and man, never lost the child-like spirit, takes by the hand and leads men as rapacious as the wolf, as treacherous as the leopard, as ferocious as the bear or the lion.

When Robert Moffat proposed to go to Africaner, the terrible demon of the Dark Continent, he was warned that he was an incarnate fiend, who would make a virtue of cruelty, and murder him that he might make a drum-head of his skin and a drinking-cup of his skull. But Moffat had faith in the gospel of the grace of God. This Hottentot chief had been driven north by Dutch invaders until, taking his refuge beyond the Orange River, he became a daring and desperate outlaw, robbing and murdering his victims, and swaying a wide region with the iron sceptre of terror. The colonial governments set a price upon his capture, dead or alive, and hired neighboring chiefs to make war upon him; but in vain. In 1818 Moffat ventured to take up his abode with Africaner. A change took place in the diabolical ruffian, so complete that it was a new creation. His outward and inward life was transformed; he became a man of peace; the helper, friend, nurse of the missionary; a student of the New Testament, an evangelist in spirit, a winner of souls. Robert Moffat's success was based on his confidence in the power of the gospel to tame the fiercest and most ferocious men, and he saw that man, who in himself combined wolf, bear, leopard, and lion, turned into a lamb.

What hope could there be of a South Sea islander who, in pure malice of cruelty, first slew his little brother without pity, and then sent the corpse to his king for a sacrifice! Dead to love, alive only to hate, making sport of murder, and murder a sport! Yet he is but a representative — as Paul would say, " a pattern" — of thousands from whom, as from him, have been cast out a legion of demons.

Sau Quala, the Karen slave, was by that same gospel brought to Christ as the first Karen convert, and then changed into an apostolic worker. He aided the missionaries in the translation of the Word, and for fifteen years guided them through the jungles in their missionary journeys in Tavoy and Mergui; then his holy zeal could no longer be pent up, and he began himself to walk through the country preaching, gathering converts, planting churches, within three years organizing nearly twenty-five hundred new disciples into over thirty congregations. His work was one of love, performed in the most heroically unselfish spirit; his voluntary poverty compelled him to leave his lovely wife behind him, because he could not afford the luxury of her companionship; and, in the face of the offer of a lucrative government position, he continued his self-denying labor, refusing to mix up secular labor with the Lord's work. Dr. Anderson closes his little biographical sketch of this Karen apostle with the exclamation, "Admirable man! Where shall we find his equal in devotion to the cause of Christ!" Yet from what depths of ignorance, selfishness, and superstition, the gospel lever lifted Sau Quala!

During the revival in Fidelia Fiske's Holyoke school in Persia, Guergis, "the vilest of the Nestorians," came to visit his daughter in the school. He was in full Koordish dress, with gun and dagger. As the girls wept and prayed, he sneered and mocked. His daughter prayed for him. He raised his fist to strike her, but the Lord held it back. Miss

Fiske sought to win him, but he continued to laugh and scorn for days. Then suddenly, as if by a lightning-stroke, he was struck down. He wept and prayed, went away to be alone with God, and came back an entirely changed man. The gun and dagger were no more to be seen. Bowed down with the weight of his sin, he declared that even " if there were no hell he could not bear such a load." He found rest in believing, and henceforth all he could say was, " My great sins and my great Saviour!" Even Miss Fiske, stunned by the miracle of such a conversion, doubted his sincerity. But until his death Deacon Guergis continued with lips and life to tell of Jesus. You might have met him travelling along the mountains, in his red trousers, striped jacket, and big turban, with Testament and hymn-book in place of gun and dagger, talking of sin and salvation, and singing with stentorian voice, " Rock of Ages," " There is a Fountain," etc. On his dying bed he would rouse up and shout, " Oh, it was free grace, free grace!"

U. Bor. Sing, the heir of the Rajah of Cherra, India, was converted by the Welsh missionaries. He was warned that in joining the Christians he would probably forfeit his right to be King of Cherra after the death of Rham Sing, who then ruled, but who, eighteen months afterward, died. The chiefs of the tribes met and unanimously decided that Bor. Sing was entitled to succeed him, but that his Christian profession stood in the way. Messenger after messenger was sent, urging him to recant. He was invited to the native council, and told that if he would put aside his religious profession they would all acknowledge him as king. His answer was: "Put aside my Christian profession? I can put aside my head-dress, or my cloak; but as for the covenant I have made with my God, I cannot for any consideration put that aside!" Another was therefore appointed king in his stead. Since then he has been impoverished by litigation about landed property, till he is now in danger of arrest and imprisonment; and Mr. Elliott, the Commissioner of Assam, has appealed to Christians in this country on his behalf. Here is a convert rejecting a crown for Christ!

Rev. John Thomas, of the Church Missionary Society, has said of a convert among the Shanars who died in 1860, that he was, without exception, the ablest and most eloquent native preacher in India. " His affection, simplicity, honesty, straightforwardness, amazing pulpit talents, and profound humility, endeared him to me more than I can describe," said this beloved missionary, who also pronounced his last sermon on the text, "enduring the cross, despising the shame," the greatest sermon he ever heard in its exaltation of Christ and its overwhelming effect.

"Blind Bartimeus," of the Hawaiian Islands, is another example of transforming grace. Out of the lowest depths of pagan vice and vileness he rose to a level with the most earnest, consecrated, self-oblivious disciples and laborers. His wonderful insight into the truth, his inspired imagination, his white-heat of ardor and fervor, his contagious enthusiasm, his passionate love for souls, enabled him to preach the most severe truths with the tenderness of a seraph; and his familiarity with the Word of God made him, blind as he was, a walking concordance.

There is not a missionary field where such triumphs of grace may not be constantly seen; transformations of character quite as marvellous and as absolutely inexplicable without a divine factor, as any miracle of apostolic days. Dr. Lindley used to say that when a native Zulu, trading some trifling article for a calico shirt, duck breeches, and a three-legged stool, got his shirt and breeches on and sat on his little stool, he was a thousand miles above all his fellows. But this is only civilization. We must follow that poor Zulu, just clothed, till the Word of God takes root in his soul, and he becomes not only beautiful and fruitful in holiness, but a preacher and a winner of souls, giving the life that has been plucked as a burning brand from the fire of an earthly hell, to be consumed on the altar of Christian service; and then we begin to understand how much farther reach the transforming influences of Christianity than those of mere civilization. The Portuguese called the Hottentots "a race of apes," and Dr. Vanderkemp read over church-doors in Cape Colony, "Dogs and Hottentots not admitted." Yet out of those Hottentots what disciples have been developed!

The Chinese in this country are the butt of ridicule and the object of contempt and violence; yet Rev. Dr. Nevius and Hunter Corbett have, with simple Chinese converts, been working wonders of evangelism that rival apostolic days. On their itinerating tours, finding a few here and there open to the gospel, they send out these new converts to tell the story to their countrymen; and so does this gospel transform the lazy, selfish, sordid Chinaman, that these missionaries find scores of lay helpers ready to give their lives to the work of gathering other converts to Christ. And so in China hundreds are every year won to Christ by lay evangelists whose whole compensation averages from three to five dollars a month!

The first messenger of Christ to carry the Bible into Korea and offer it to the King was a Chinese convert. The noblest examples of self-denial, separation unto God, passion for souls, singleness of aim, evangelistic zeal, and liberal systematic giving, which have been found during this century, have been the outgrowth of missionary fields, and often of the most hopeless soil, previously rank with every unholy product. The new converts from the most degraded tribes have often put to shame the ripest fruits of our Christian civilization!

In January, 1872, during the week of prayer, one or two Japanese converts, recently brought to Christ and taught in the private classes of the missionaries, came into the English meeting at Yokohama. There they heard read and expounded, the story of that first Pentecost from the Book of the Acts of the Apostles. As though themselves set on fire with pentecostal flames, they fell on their knees, and with prayers like those of Daniel and Paul, besought God to pour out the Spirit in a new Pentecost upon Japan, till even the captains of the English and American war-ships wept and said, " The prayers of these new Japanese converts take the heart out of us."

In a personal communication to the author, the Rev. William Ashmore, D.D., of Swatow, China, writes, as to the signs of divine grace among the Chinese : —

" *Bring of the fish which ye have now caught.*"

" The converts give evidence, all-sufficient, that they are of the kind the Master takes to Himself, and not those which are thrown away. Conversion in China is followed by exactly the same fruits as in all the rest of the world. Love to all the saints they evince in word and in deed. Next to the love of Christ, which reigns supreme, this sympathy and large-hearted active charity to persecuted brethren in other places is noteworthy. Before conversion they cared nothing about suffering people elsewhere ; but now, hearing that some whom they have never seen are driven from their homes for Christ's sake, they are ready to share with them what little they have.

"'The crucial test of a man's faith in China is his repudiation of ancestral worship for himself after death. An old Christian called his idol-worshipping sons to his bedside, and, gathering all his remaining strength in one last effort, charged them to send for the Christians to read the Scriptures at his funeral, and pray and sing about the resurrection, and, under pain of his displeasure, have no heathen ceremonies over him and no offerings made to him after he was gone. Knowing their perversity, he even threatened that if any heathen rites should disgrace his burial, and the Lord would permit, his spirit would come back and manifest his abhorrence. Another, a poor woman, after asking for prayer and rendering up her own praise, handed me the savings of a lifetime, — more than two hundred dollars, — begging me to use them for Jesus. The last request of her husband was, that when his tomb should be made, there might be written upon it simply his name, and after it, 'a disciple of Jesus.' Having been a faithful witness in his life, he wished to continue witnessing after his death."

Let these few individual examples, drawn from the sable sons of Africa, the Karen slaves of Burmah, the wild Koords of Persia, the superstitious Brahmins of India, the vile pagans of Polynesia, the iron-bound Confucianists of China, and the benighted Buddhists of Japan, stand as illustrations of the fact that wherever the gospel goes, its career is one of conquest. God is with His own Word, and it returns not to Him void.

CHAPTER XXIV.

THE PRODUCTS OF GOD'S HUSBANDRY.

WE turn from individual examples of the fruits of grace on heathen soil to consider a few of the broader fields, which have brought forth some thirty, some sixty, and some even an hundred fold under God's gracious tillage. If the conversion and sanctification of individuals is a remarkable proof of divine power, what shall be said of communities where the whole aspect and prospect of affairs have been not only rapidly, but radically, transformed!

In 1816 William A. B. Johnson, a plain German laborer, went from London, as a school-teacher, to Sierra Leone. When he first went to Regent's Town he found a thousand people saved from the holds of slave-ships; they were wild and naked, represented twenty-two hostile tribes, and seemed absolutely beyond reformation. They had no morals, but were shiftless, brutal thieves and murderers, crowding together in filthy huts, without even the conception of marriage; and as to religion, that was devil-worship. Johnson cast himself on that gospel which is the power and the wisdom of God unto salvation, and before one year had passed, old and young began to inquire after salvation; the woods heard their whispered prayers, and the hills echoed with their hymns. The whole aspect of the settlement was changed. Trades and even learned professions took the place of lawlessness and violence; idleness and ignorance gave way to industry and intelligence. They built a stone church, which was regularly filled with nearly two thousand worshippers, and schools were crowded with children. Marriage took the place of promiscuous concubinage; the Lord's Supper displaced heathen revels; and thievery, profanity, and blasphemy ceased. All this Johnson saw, yet he died in 1823. All this change was the fruit of seven years.

The existing Christian community in Turkey is an unanswerable proof of what the gospel can do, even in soil as hopeless as that of the Sultan's dominions. Here are exhibited the fruits of the Spirit in superior intelligence and integrity, morality and spirituality, Christian activity and benevolence. Wheeler's " Ten Years on the Euphrates " is one of the most thrilling books in our missionary library. It shows us how, along the great river Euphrates, scores of self-supporting churches have been planted, sustaining their own native pastors, and demonstrating the practicability of the tithe-system as the financial basis of evangelization. Some of these churches began with but ten believers; but each conscientiously gave his tithe, and these ten tithes constituted a sum, equal to the average income of those poor church-members, to support a pastor willing to live on a level with his people, and leaving him his tithe likewise to offer to the Lord, and yet have as much as they for his own use.

And so from the Tigris to the Bosphorus, in face of the despotic oppression and persecuting hostility of the Turkish government, Protestant churches have not only been organized, and have outlived all hinderances to life and growth, but have waxed strong wrestling with the storm; and it is hoped that these churches in the Ottoman Empire will soon be able to dismiss missionary oversight and take care of their own Christian work, not only self-supporting and self-governing, but self-propagating.

The "Lone Star" Mission among the Telugus has for eight years been the cynosure of all eyes. At one time it had almost ceased to shine, however feebly; then it suddenly blazed forth with a brilliancy like that of Sirius. At the anniversary meetings in Albany, N. Y., in 1853, it was proposed to abandon this mission, as both a fruitless and hopeless enterprise. At least thirteen years seemed to have been spent in vain. On that occasion

Dr. S. F. Smith wrote and published the poem beginning

> "Shine on, Lone Star! thy radiance bright
> Shall yet illume the western sky," etc.

Twenty-five years passed away, and the eventful year 1878 came. In that same "Lone Star" Mission there was a display of divine grace that has had no parallel since the first Pentecost. A spiritual harvest was there gathered which seemed to many incredible. Within twenty-one days there were added to one church in Ongole 5,429 new converts, and on one day, 2,222. Still later, in that same field, there were 3,262 additional baptisms, making the whole number baptized from June 16 to July 31, — forty-five days, — nearly 9,000! probably exceeding the harvest of the first Pentecost. That church in Ongole was organized in 1867, only eleven years before, with eight souls. In those eleven years every one of those little ones literally "became a thousand." (Isa. lx. 22; Ps. lxxii. 16.)

Nor were these converts hastily gathered or carelessly admitted. The severe famine of 1877 had made the feeding of the starving the work of the mission. And lest any should be moved to join the mission church from mercenary motives, and because there was neither time nor strength to examine candidates, those who applied for baptism were kept waiting till the pressure of famine was relieved. In fact, not one hundred of the number received ever had from the missionaries the value of a quarter of a cent. As we look back, we see that these fruits, instead of being overstated, are understated. Sixty thousand people during that memorable year turned to the living God from vain idols in Southern India.

What a white harvest field may be found in the empire of Japan! That edict against Christianity has never been repealed, and yet what headway the gospel has made there, overcoming even opposition! At first, only secular teaching was permitted; then, as this Christian teaching more and more savored of the salt of the gospel, it was tolerated; then preaching in private was followed by assemblies for Christian worship and the organization of Christian churches. In 1865 the first convert was enrolled. In March, 1872, the first Christian congregation of Yokohama was formed with eleven members,—the first-fruits of the prayers of those few Japanese in the week of prayer just before. Within ten years those eleven have multiplied one hundred-fold. In October, 1880, the natives held a meeting in the open air on the grounds of a hotel in the public park at Uyeno; some four or five thousand people were in attendance, and the meeting lasted two days. It was openly advertised in the native newspapers, and publicly announced by large post-bills, which met the eye everywhere, and one of them on the very spot where the old edict board had so long stood. The mighty momentum of the gospel is felt even by the government, and before it even the spirit of opposition is giving way. Japan has been taken possession of by the Church of Christ, and the key to that Sunrise Kingdom is the common school.

The changes in the Japanese Empire are far more rapid and radical than we appreciate; and they are triumphs not of civilization only, but of Christianity. Fukuzawa, in advocating the adoption of the Christian religion by the State as a measure of political advancement, may disavow all personal adhesion to it as a disciple; but his two sons are at Oberlin, and are Christians. The natives, even the most educated, cannot but feel the superiority of the gospel to their heathen systems; and they marvel as they see how, without even naming an idol, Christian disciples have a "splendid way of dying." At Kioto, the priests organized a Society of Natural Religion, to oppose Christianity, and called it the "Yaso Taiji;" but the government forbade the use of the obnoxious word "Taiji," as implying an intention of violent antagonism. The priests may conspire to oppose, but the religion of Christ is laying hold of the people.

Dr. Hepburn thinks that, if all foreign missionaries were expelled to-morrow, the natives would carry on the work. It is said that in one district, since 1873, seventy-one Buddhist temples have been abandoned to secular uses, and since 1871 seven hundred throughout the empire.

At the meeting of the American Board at Syracuse in 1879 President Seelye moved the following deliverance: —

"Never before has the gospel wrought such great and speedy changes as during the past seven years in Japan. It is not only the most remarkable chapter in the history of modern missions, but there is nothing in the history of the world to compare with it. We talk about the early triumphs of Christianity, but the early records of the Church, bright as they may be, pale in the light of what is taking place before our eyes at the present time. Even Madagascar offers nothing to compare with Japan."

Japan possesses two thousand newspapers, — all the outgrowth of twenty-five years, — more than Italy, or Austria, or Spain and

Russia combined, and twice as many as all Asia beside. Scholars of Europe and Japan are making a new alphabet of Roman letters to represent the eight thousand Japanese characters; a Japanese-Latin lexicon has been made, and Japanese-English books are now preparing. In Fukuzawa's school at Tokio a missionary is teaching, and Bible doctrine is prominent. Fifteen students recently asked baptism. We do not appreciate the rapid elimination of the Asiatic features from the government, and of the antiquated Oriental ideas from the popular mind. The entire New Testament is now given to the people in their own tongue, and the Bible societies are scattering the leaves of the Tree of Life; the Christian press is filling the land with a Christian literature; schools are gathering both boys and girls, and there are three theological seminaries; and the Island Empire adopts a Christian type of civilization.

Mr. Tamura, a Japanese now in America, acknowledges the fivefold debt which Japan owes to this country: 1. The opening of that island empire to the world.   2. The influence of America on the political life of Japan. 3. The pattern furnished for her educational system.   4. The aid given to Japan in securing an international standing.   5. The introduction of Christianity.   Upon this last " debt " he expatiates in no ordinary terms.   He says that the empire was like a decaying tree, whose fruit was cruelty, bloodshed, and corruption.   "Even hope was dead.   In 1859 the sower came, bearing the seed of truth and life and hope.   The Sun of Righteousness began to shine, and the dark clouds of Shintooism, Confucianism, and Buddhism began to melt away."   He testifies to the wonderful rapidity with which the gospel roots itself in the soil of Japan.   "During the last ten years over one hundred churches organized; over eight thousand souls saved.   The evangelization of Japan is at hand."   Thus while sceptical travellers are reviling and ridiculing the work of missions, the natives of these lands are loud-voiced in testimony to their value.

We have already seen how difficult a field

China presented for even a divine husbandry. Missionaries labored in Foochow for thirty years, among two millions of people. Eleven years of that thirty left behind not one convert, and scarce a visible token of good, to reward all the labor and prayer expended. Even the Church Missionary Society said, "There are no results that justify the continuance of the mission." But Mr. Wolfe, their missionary, said, "I will not give up this work;" and a few months later the first convert was baptized, then three more, and, eighteen years after, there were three thousand native disciples in Foochow. Ten years ago it was reported that there were over three hundred Protestant churches, with fifteen thousand members and fifty thousand adherents; and these congregations, rapidly advancing towards self-support, contributing $20,000 annually. The appetite for reading is such that the Chinese fight each other in their eagerness to seize tracts distributed among them by the missionaries; and in one year the mission presses at Shanghai yielded to the Presbyterian Board five per cent upon the whole amount spent that year for all its missions throughout the world. A whole town of five hundred inhabitants is lately reported as embracing Christianity.

In Sanui, eighty miles from Canton, an unsuccessful endeavor was made to get control of a spacious temple; it was refused at any price. Three years after it was *offered* for the nominal price of twenty dollars a year; and now the native pastor, Lai Pot Sün, is there gathering his flock.

In British Columbia, on Pacific shores, William Duncan, out of a body of brutal Indians, some of them cannibals, built his Metlakahtla, a Christian state, which, not only morally and religiously, but socially, politically, and commercially, is a new crown for our Lord and King. After six months' study of their language he made his first sermon. Nine tribes crowded that one village, and he could not get them to come together, in the same meeting; so he preached that first sermon nine times in one evening.

As long ago as 1880 he stood at the head of a community of one thousand souls, with the largest church north of San Francisco, and manse, school, shops, and all the marks of a Christian civilization. He is solving the problem of the Indian question, and proving that the decay of these aboriginal tribes may not only be arrested, but give place to the ingrafted scion of gospel life. Lord Dufferin could not gather from all the rich resources of the dead and living languages, which his silver tongue so grandly uses, words fit to express his astonishment at what he saw in this community. Surely it is better and cheaper to evangelize the Indians than to exterminate them. General Sherman's campaign against the Cheyennes is reported to have cost $5,000,000; it costs $500,000 to kill an Indian, and $500 to convert one. Those who estimate every question on a financial basis may do well to consider these comparative figures. History may yet prove that there are some "good Indians" who are not "dead Indians."

All these examples might be multiplied absolutely without limit.   There is not a field of missions, the world over, where the unmistakable fruits of grace have not been made to grow and thrive.   The Spirit of God moves over the abyss of paganism, and divine life develops in a new creation.

CHAPTER XXV.

POLYNESIA has been the scene of gospel triumphs which, for character, frequency, and rapidity, scarce admit of comparison. Here is a sort of submerged continent whose numberless projections form islands in the Pacific, and wherever the gospel touches these islands it works wonderful changes in their civil and social life.

The story of the Sandwich Islands, or Hawaiian group, is too familiar to need repetition. Within fifty years an entire people, saved from extinction, took their place in the great brotherhood of Christian nations side by side with others, on the same plane of civilization, and in the same work of evangelization. This shining example of the dynamics of the gospel prepared us to look for similar conquests, which singularly enough have been specially multiplied among the islands of the sea.

The annals of the gospel in the South Seas should be written in starlight, for they include some of the most shining pages in the history of missions. John Williams, the blacksmith's boy, the apostle of Polynesia, found idolatry and savagery of the worst type and lowest grade. Yet his progress was one rapid career of conquest. Churches and schools grew, he knew not how. A lawless people adopt courts, frame a code of laws, and conduct trials by jury. Printing-presses scatter the leaves of the Tree of Life; and a missionary society is formed, with Pomare as its first president, and $2,500 are its first year's contribution. Within one year after he landed at Raratonga, the population of the whole Hervey group, numbering seven thousand, have thrown away their idols, and a church building six hundred feet long is erecting. He turns to the Samoa group, and shortly has the whole people, numbering sixty thousand, gathered in Christian schools. Pomare, Queen of Tahiti and Moorea, died at seventy years of age. At her birth the missionaries had just come to the South Sea Islands. Not one convert had been made. At her death more than three hundred islands were evangelized.

In the New Hebrides, John Geddie's marble slab bears the expressive, laconic epitaph, and epitome of his experience at Aneityum:

> "When he came here,
>   He found no Christians;
> When he left,
>   He left no heathens."

The Fiji group may perhaps challenge any other record of gospel transformation and triumph, in any age or land, to outshine the golden pages of its history. In fifty years, changes have taken place which no pen of man can fitly portray. The condition of the islands when, fifty years ago, missionaries first landed in Lakemba, was simply horrible. Two hundred thousand people were living in such a death-shade, that cannibalism was a requirement of their religion. Infanticide, strangling of widows, tribal wars, atrocious cruelties, were common and awakened no repulsion. If a chief built his hut, he surrounded the piles on which it rested by rows of human beings, buried alive. If he launched a canoe, the rollers by which it was borne to the sea were living bodies, crushed and ground to a jelly by its weight.

The story of Fiji would fill a volume, but language has no adequate terms to describe the abasement of this people, nor their atrocious and abominable customs. Such deeds of darkness should be written in blood and registered in hell. The Fijians are now a Christian people. In seven years after missionary labor began among them, the island of Ono had not one heathen left upon it, and had become the " light-bearer " to the whole group.

But at least the outlines of this marvellous romance of missions should be drawn.

Against such colossal and gigantic diabolism as seldom confronts even a missionary in pagan lands, in the name of Jesus, and with faith in his presence and power, two British Wesleyan missionaries, — Rev. William Cross and David Cargill, — Oct. 12, 1835, undertook to open a mission. They gave the Fijians a grammar and dictionary of their own tongue, and the Gospel according to St. Matthew. Within eight months the new gospel held sufficient sway to prevent the cruel rites of cannibalism upon the shipwrecked crew of the " Active." The missionary band grew, and the sway of the gospel extended; cannibalism, murder, war, and finally polygamy, gave way before it; hundreds and thousands of native converts were gathered into Christian churches; idolatry was abolished, houses of Christian worship were built, and schools organized. The whole aspect of the islands was changed. And at the fiftieth anniversary, in October, 1885, there were over 1,200 chapels; a total of 2,350 missionaries, native ministers, teachers, and preachers; over 26,000 communicants and 4,600 probationers, and over 42,000 Sunday-school scholars. Every village has its Christian churches, schools, and homes, and there are more families that observe family prayer and attend public worship than in the most enlightened centres of Christendom.

One indication may be given of the progress of the gospel in Fiji. In the ancient Fijian city of Bau stands a stone with a history like that of Moloch. It stood in front of the chief temple, Vata mi Tawaki, which, on a high foundation, towered above the many shrines and fanes of Bau. The corpses destined for cannibal orgies, trailed in their gore along the dusty soil, were dashed by the head against this stone, as an offering to the divinities, before being devoured. For at least thirty years — since cannibalism fell before the power of Christianity — this stone has had upon it no stain of human blood, and now is converted into a baptismal font.

With the consent and co-operation of the chief, this weird relic of the past has been borne from the spot which it had occupied, and set up in the great Bau church. Here a cavity was hollowed out in it, and thus it was changed into a font, with associations such as few church fonts possess. Curiosity-hunters complain of the removal of this heathen monument, as the further carrying away of the stone in pieces is prevented; but the history of this fragment, and the contrast of its past and its present position and uses, throw much light on what mission work has done in Fiji.

The Samoa group, or Navigator's Islands, is in Central Polynesia, about ten degrees below the equator, three thousand miles east of Australia, and perhaps one fifth as far northeast of Fiji. When first found, the natives were the lowest, worst savages. "Massacre Bay," by its name, records the cruel slaughter of twelve white men by them, in La Perouse's expedition in 1787. Williams and Barff, first missionaries to the group, and representing the London Society, landed there in 1830. The transformations effected within these fifty-five years seem incredible.

The Scriptures were translated, so that within thirty years the people were all nominally Christian, and had in their hands an octavo reference Bible in their own tongue; and for all Bibles or other books they were taught to pay. Within seven years after the Bible issued from the press, an edition of ten thousand copies was exhausted, and the entire outlay of over $15,000 was repaid by the sales. Another and revised edition equally large is exhausted. When the mission began, money was unknown to the Samoans; now four nations are represented in mercantile business, and a trade with the natives, worth from a quarter to a half million dollars, is annually carried on in the shops.

Of a population of thirty-five thousand, there are now six thousand converted men and women, and as many more who in the same faith have fallen asleep. Eight thousand children are in the schools; and Dr. Turner says there are not probably twenty houses all over the group in which you would not find the Word of God and daily family worship.

Thousands of pages of Christian and educational literature are in circulation. At Malua, on the island of Upolu, is a mission seminary now over forty years old, supported by the students themselves, who give up an hour or two daily, and the whole of each Wednesday and the first Monday of each month, to industrial pursuits. The seminary has a sea frontage, so that the students may fish; and their plantations abound with fruit and vegetables, pigs and poultry. The only expense to the London Society has been the salaries of the two teachers, and the institution now owns an estate worth $50,000, and has over eighty pupils. So popular is this seminary, that there are two or three applicants for every vacancy; and young men have come from nineteen other islands. Within twenty years the native churches, beside the support of their own native pastors, have contributed on an average $6,000 per year to the London Society. Where can Christendom exhibit a half-century of work more prolific in fruits?

The late Charles Darwin, the naturalist, in early life visited the island of Terra del Fuego, and described the inhabitants as the most degraded and brutal people living on the earth; in many respects worse than the brutes. A Scottish captain, Allen Gardner, went there three times to carry them the bread of life, but finally perished of starvation, with all his followers. When his dead body was discovered they found inscribed on the rocks above his head the words of the Psalmist: "My soul, wait thou only on the Lord, for my expectation is from Him;" and his "expectations" have been fulfilled, and a marvellous work of grace accomplished. So much so, that when Mr. Darwin visited the island again — a short time before his death — he became satisfied of the power of the gospel to redeem even the most savage tribes, although he had been an unbeliever in Christianity.

Thomas Powell placed on the little island of Nanumaga a native evangelist. He found the island full of idols of stone and wood, altars in every house, and temples almost as many as dwellings. He was kept two hours on the beach while the priests, with absurd rites, sought to avert the wrath of their gods for allowing the stranger to land. The men and women were almost as nude as the children, and made a virtue of nakedness. Eight years afterward, one third of the entire population were members of the Christian church, and two-thirds of the children were in Christian schools; and those new church members have contributed to the support of the gospel and its extension an average of $1.60 each. Not an idol is now to be found, nor an idol temple, and the people are all clothed decently, and sit with delight to listen to the gospel.

In all these cases the lowest type of paganism was confronted. The people seemed sunk so low as to have scarce mind or manhood to grasp the simplest Christian truths. But the Spirit of God has demonstrated that it is both a fallacy and a heresy to affirm that any human being is too degraded to be made a new man in Christ Jesus, a new creation in which old things pass away and all things become new.

Look at Madagascar! The French governor of the island of Bourbon told the first Protestant missionaries to that country that they might as well try to convert cattle, as to make Christians of the Malagasy. Madagascar stands now the miracle of modern missions, "the crown of the London Missionary Society," promising to be to the Dark Continent what England is to Europe, — an evangelizing centre. The gospel barely got a foothold when a Neronian persecution met it with the black flag that meant "no quarter;" but twenty-five years failed to dislodge it by fire or blood. And a few years ago the Queen issued a proclamation in the name of God declaring Christianity the law of her realm, built a chapel for Christian worship within court grounds, and celebrated with her people a fortnight of jubilee. The

Malagasy "cattle" have "developed" in an incredibly short period into intelligent Christian disciples. No period of Christian history can probably show more fruits or better fruits of thirty-five years of missionary labor, than in Madagascar.

And so Christlieb says: "The most degraded of heathen nations may be brought to listen, and learn to believe. We have thus the comforting assurance that no race is so spiritually dead that by the good news it cannot rise to newness of life, no tongue so barbarian that it will not admit of a translation of the Bible, no heathen soul so sunk that he cannot become a new creature in Christ Jesus."

Truly the gospel needs no apologetics amid such displays of its dynamics. While it is the power of God unto salvation to every one that believeth, Jew or Greek, barbarian, Scythian, bond or free, who shall be "ashamed of the gospel of Christ?" The civilization and evangelization of these islands, within half a century, furnish a mightier defence of our faith than all the apologies of the ages.

CHAPTER XXVI.

ANOTHER of the "gracious signs" of the presence and power of God in connection with the work of missions, a special seal and sanction set upon the work, may be found in the peculiar consecration of character developed in the workmen who have heartily entered into this great harvest-field.

Science, that interpreter of nature, shows us the crystal and the cell, her miracles of inorganic symmetry and of organic life. But God's Spirit, that interpreter of grace, reveals to us greater marvels in holy lives that to the beauty of the crystal add the energy of the cell, and shine not with a cold, imprisoned lustre, but with the light and life and love of God. " History is philosophy teaching by examples," said Dionysius of Halicarnassus. To appreciate the divine spirit of missions, we need to study the missionary biography, which teaches by examples its power to illumine and transfigure human character. What an alphabet is that which presents such names as Abeel, Ashmore, Barnes, Boardman, Brainerd, Burns, Bushnell, Carey, Crowther, Dober, Duff, Edwards, Egede, Eliot, Ellis, Farman, Fiske, Geddie, Goodell, Goodale, Grant, Greig, Gutzlaff, Gulick, Harms, Hannington, Henderson, Hepburn, Jessup, Judson, Kiernander, Krapf, Lindley, Livingstone, McAll, Marshman, Martyn, Mayhew, Milne, Moffat, Morrison, Newell, Newton, Owen, Oncken, Perkins, Plutschau, Rhea, Riggs, Ross, Scudder, Stoddard, Schmidt, Schwartz, Spangenberg, Eli Smith, Taylor, Turner, Van Dyke, Ward, Williams, Wolff, Xavier, Ziegenbalg, Zeisberger, Zinzendorf, and a legion beside, whose lives constitute new chapters in the acts of the apostles, and both demonstrate and illustrate that true apostolic succession of a Christ-like spirit and a Pauline enthusiasm and self-oblivion!

Sir R. Temple, late Governor of Bombay, says: —

"Of all departments I have ever administered, none have been more efficiently or economically conducted than that of missions; and of all the officers I have commanded, no better body of men have I known than the missionaries."

In a letter written by Robert N. Cust, Esq., and addressed to the American Board meeting at Boston in 1885, and published in the "Missionary Herald," appears the following passage. The whole Church may well be proud of such a testimony.

"The missionary appears to me to be the *highest type of human excellence in the nineteenth century, and his profession to be the noblest.* He has the enterprise of the merchant, without the narrow desire of gain; the dauntlessness of the soldier, without the shedding of blood; the zeal of the geographical explorer, but for a higher motive than science. Now, if there is anything greater than an English missionary, it is an American. My words may be read on both sides of the Atlantic, and I write them deliberately ; if my convictions were the other way, I should not hesitate to express them. I knew John Newton, of Lahore, forty years ago, and I know him still. I knew Farman, and Barnes, and Joseph Owen, and many of the Episcopalian-Methodist Mission, more than twenty-five years ago in India, and Van Dyke, and Eli Smith, and Robinson, — the Palestine explorer, — at the same period. Later on, I have made the acquaintance of the great army of American missionaries at Constantinople, Beirût, and in Egypt. I infringed on Labaree at Tiflis, in South Russia. Many American missionaries, starting to Africa, have come to see me in London, and I have taken note of their character and calibre. I have lived among missionaries of my own country all that period, and know members of all denominations. *They are the salt of the earth.*"

These words of Mr. Cust are abundantly authorized by the entire history of missions. Paul's self-denial and self-forgetfulness, patience in suffering and passion for souls, ardor and fervor, earnestness and enthusiasm, holiness and heroism, are only the anticipation and illustration of the divine virtues exemplified in the noble army of missionary martyrs from his day until now. Every field of labor and every age of history repeat the testimony that there is something in missionary work that both demands and develops the highest type of manhood and womanhood.

Here is the reason why the Word of God and the man of God must go together: the personal witness found in the man is as needful in its way as the inspired witness found in the message. It was Morrison himself that was the Chinese bible; it was Mrs. Grant that compelled even the Nestorian bishops to confess the empty shell of their formalism, and bury her sacred dust, as the temple of the Holy Ghost, in the very floor of their holy place; it was Mrs. Judson that won the Burmese — who kissed her shadow as she passed — to believe in the religion that could shape such symmetrical womanhood. Eliot's utter self-abnegation and David Brainerd's martyr spirit made them almost objects of worship with the Indians, as Dr. Hogg was mourned as a father by the natives all along the Nile, and Livingstone, by the sable sons of the South. Christianity has somehow produced her ripest fruits, and the ripest fruits of manhood and womanhood, in mission fields; and there must be something in this work that makes heroes and martyrs.

Even the flaming zeal of Xavier is matched by the heroism of Rosine Krapf, going with her husband into the heart of Abyssinia, sharing all the exposures and privations of his flight, though even then overshadowed by the approach of that sacred primal sorrow of her sex. Under the shade of a tree in the wilderness of Shoho he took the dying babe in his arms to dedicate it to the Triune God. Hear her, in her own suffering, seeking to comfort him, naming that child of sorrow by the Amharic name for a "tear;" then valiantly accompanying her husband through perils of land and water, sharing with him shipwreck; and when dying, with her last breath enjoining him to bear her body to the African shores, that her grave might remind the pagan Wanikas what had brought her to that land, and might inspire other missionaries to bear the fiery cross through the Galla country into Abyssinia. If the annals of history furnish any examples of more heroic self-oblivion, what are they?

In South Africa there was established a hospital for lepers, and in connection with it a large piece of ground enclosed by a wall, and containing fields which the lepers cultivated. There was only one entrance, and those who entered in by that gate were not allowed to go out. Inside were multitudes of lepers in all stages of their loathsome disease. Two Moravian missionaries, filled with heavenly love and anxious to carry the tidings of joy to those in such misery, chose the lazar-house as their field of labor. They entered it, never to come out again; and when they died there were other missionaries ready to take their places. Surely these men followed Him who died for us while we were yet sinners.

Livingstone, in Africa, was thirty-nine times attacked with fever, driven northward by persecution, yet never giving up, and dying on his knees, of sheer exhaustion. Dober and his co-laborers at St. Thomas were told that they could not preach to those ignorant slaves. "Then we will sell ourselves as slaves, and preach while we work by their side."

The Japanese, impressed with the superiority of a Christian civilization, and especially of our common schools, sent for one of our missionaries and asked him to take the superintendence of education throughout the empire of Japan; and he said, "Gentlemen, I have not time to take the superintendence of your schools; I have given myself to the preaching of the gospel and the translation of the Word of God, and I cannot undertake secular instruction;" and he declined a princely salary that he might carry on his work.

The reason for the development of such a type of character in missionaries is not an obscure one. If the missionary workman is inspired to heroism by providential signals, still grander, if possible, is the inspiration of gracious signs. He ventures into the wildest and worst wastes of the pagan world. In that soil grows every product, — earthly, sensual, devilish. Not only is the image of God defaced and almost effaced, but the image of man is so shattered and wrecked that the "humanity" upon which he labors is literally like the beasts that perish. Woman is a tool, a slave, a victim; home is an earthly hell. Even language is so degraded that it has no words or phrases fit to express or convey spiritual ideas and conceptions. Out of that soil nothing has grown for a thousand years but the rankest, deadliest vices, lusts, crimes, that provoke even the patience of God to burn up the whole harvest of evil with the fires of His holy wrath.

In the midst of such society the humble preacher or teacher sows the seed of the kingdom; and, sooner or later, the plants of grace begin to grow and thrive; they spread, they crowd out the gigantic growths of sin and superstition, until, where the Devil's harvest-field was, appears the garden of the Lord, with every characteristic fruit of godliness abounding, blooming and fragrant. The heathen soil supports a Christian community.

What would induce such men as Schwartz and Carey, Morrison and Judson, Oncken and Lindley, Jessup and Taylor, McAll and Hannington, to leave their work? To have such signals of Providence to guide and guard, and such signs of grace to inspire and encourage, is ample compensation for all the toil, trial, peril, and privation of a missionary life in the deserts of paganism, the land of the shadow of death!

CHAPTER XXVII.

THE ASPECT AND PROSPECT.

A RAPID glance around the whole field shows us the world open in all directions to Christian missions, and if every energy were put forth, we can do no more than occupy the fields ready for the sower with his seed, and in many cases for the reaper with his sickle.

1. Paganism is manifestly in a state of decadence. Pagan peoples have lost, or are losing, faith in their idols and superstitions. The gospel has proven itself able to reach and to save both the lowest and the highest of the heathen. Its divine lever is lifting whole nations to a higher level of intellectual, moral, and social life; overturning antiquated customs and deep-rooted errors; purifying the marriage relation and establishing the family;

emphasizing the dignity of man and the social equality of woman; abolishing caste and slavery; and demolishing idols and turning idol fanes into houses of Christian worship.

Even merchants and political economists confess that, if Christian missions do no more, they civilize and educate. In England, Rev. C. Jukes, of Madagascar, stated that though, sixty years since, no one in that island could read, now three hundred thousand can read; and most of them possess at least a part of the Bible. For every missionary to the South Seas, from fifty thousand to one hundred thousand dollars annually return in the channels of trade; and even Charles Darwin contributed to the London Missionary Society on the score of philanthropy and political economy.

2. Mohammedanism has thus far proven the most stubborn foe of the gospel, and, as yet, its territory remains almost intact. Yet there are hopeful features even here, for, being both monotheistic and iconoclastic, it is the foe of polytheism and idolatry, and, therefore, so far the ally of Christianity. The very

restrictions surrounding the Koran help to make one Arabic version of the Bible reach people of many diverse nations and tongues.

Just now, especially in Syria and Turkey, there are signs all around the horizon that even the rigid resistance of Moslem bigotry is relaxing; and direct efforts to evangelize the followers of Islam will at once be made. The United Presbyterians, so successful among the Copts in Egypt, have also done much good work, and are likely to do more, among Mohammedans. Already, in their schools, one in seven is from this class.

3. Papacy shows an entire change of attitude toward the gospel. The "twelve hundred and sixty" years seem expired; the wall of adamant beyond which, for so long a time, evangelical teachers and preachers could not pass without daring the rack and the stake, the dungeons of the Inquisition and the anathemas of the Pope, — that wall has breaches so many and broad that gates of steel no longer avail. Sixteen years ago the temporal power of the Pope was broken, and

now the spiritual sceptre is loosely held. France welcomes McAll's gospel stations, and Italy and Spain admit Bibles and Protestant preachers; while in the Eternal City itself, Protestant chapels lift their spires, like fingers, in solemn menace, in sight of St. Peter's great cathedral.

4. The Jews are now attracting the eyes of the nations. Some years since there was a powerful awakening among them in North Africa; hundreds and even thousands of them are among the converts in England, America, and Europe. Good work has been done for them in Persia; and under Rabinowitz, in Russia, there has been for two years a gathering of God's ancient people into New Testament brotherhoods of a unique type, and in large numbers. We account this last as one of the most startling signs of the times. The fulness of the Gentiles may soon be come in, and God's ancient Israel may once more be graffed into their own olive-tree.

Such is the general outlook. It will be observed that throughout these pages we have laid but little stress upon mere numbers. Figures belong to the changeable and changing factors in missions, and we prefer to deal in the great permanent facts and principles which underlie what is transient. Moreover, no adequate idea of the work done is conveyed by the numerical increase of converts, or even of stations.

Some who antagonize missions, and aim to belittle their success, claim that such figures mislead by exaggerating the facts; that these converts are often ignorant, superstitious, half-converted or not at all, actuated by mercenary or selfish motives, or are at best unstable. Granting all this, yet in the most favored Christian land and churches just such conditions prevail; and careful comparison shows that the proportion of converts who prove unworthy and unstable is smaller in heathen than in Christian lands. The difficulties and dangers, which these native converts have to face, test their sincerity and render them courageous and constant in their adhesion to Christ.

But more than this we may safely say. We

do not place much value upon the number of converts reported, because it actually *understates the progress of the gospel.* A few only have the courage to confess faith in Christ; while hundreds have lost faith in idol gods and poetic myths, or cherish a secret hope, which only a death-bed may reveal. Statistics may give us the number of Christian churches and converts, schools and pupils; but there are facts which have no report or record, but which are quite as important. Dr. Ashmore says that while converts count only as individuals, the great masses of the heathen are sceptical about their systems. The confidence of vast numbers, in the creeds and customs and fables in which they have been trained, is undermined, and they are like the Midianites, who found in their own dreams an ominous prophecy of their defeat before Gideon. { God is honeycombing Satan's " Hell-gate," and a violent, sudden, explosive upheaval is coming; and the heathen themselves have apprehensions of the approaching crisis. }

Still further, every church gathered out of a Pagan or Moslem community represents a widely pervasive Christian atmosphere. Each mission station is a centre of light, radiating in every direction redeeming influences; each native church is the centre of a Christian community closely identified with Christianity. If there be two million converts, there are perhaps two hundred million to whom the knowledge of the gospel and its transforming power have more or less reached.

Here again are facts which no figures show, no reports reveal. Light diminishes darkness which it does not dispel. Sir Bartle Frère says that the general extension of even a superficial acquaintance with Christianity "sounds the death-knell of caste." An acute observer of Africa's history finds the slave-trade giving way everywhere in proportion to the preaching of the gospel. Pagan institutions cannot stand firm when Christian women penetrate to the zenanas, and Christian schools bend the twig that is to determine the inclination of the tree. In India, schools that numbered thirteen in 1861, counted thirteen hundred in 1883. Buddhist temples in Siam are furnishing materials for houses of prayer to the true God; and in sheer despair there is an attempt to fuse all pagan faiths, to prevent the extinction of all.

In Syria, where every obstacle seemed to exclude the gospel, education was the potent key that unlocked the iron gates. Hundreds of Protestant schools, with thousands of pupils, — half of them girls, and one tenth of those girls Mohammedans, — cannot fail to change the entire conditions of society. A Mohammedan pasha himself told Mrs. Thompson that schools like hers made impossible another massacre like that of Mount Lebanon in 1860; for all sects are there gathered, and the children of the murdered sit side by side with those of the murderers, and grow up together.

We have heard of an English colonel who, though a resident in India, "saw and shot thirty tigers, but never saw a convert;" we have also heard of a devoted missionary in

India who never saw one tiger, but spent his life among converts; and we conclude that each saw what he chose to see. Tigers are not generally found on the mission premises, nor converts in the jungles; but either tigers or converts may be found if you *go where they are.*

A blue-book is the last place in the world where one might expect to find appreciative testimony in favor of mission work; and yet such appreciative testimony actually occurs in the Blue-Book of the Government of India, just published.   In speaking of the missionaries it says: —

" No statistics can give a fair view of all that they have done. The moral tone of their preaching is recognized by hundreds who do not follow them as converts. The lessons which they inculcate have given to the people new ideas, not only on purely religious questions, but on the nature of evil, the obligations of law, and the motives by which human conduct should be regulated. Insensibly, a higher standard of moral conduct is becoming familiar to the people."[1]

[1] New York Tribune, July 25, 1886.

The aspect is encouraging; the prospect is as bright as prophecy and promise can make it. Triumphs are before the Great Conqueror, whose glory will outshine all previous victories. That *annus mirabilis* of modern missionary history is itself both a prophecy and a foretaste of coming times of refreshing. During that one year, and in the land which is the key to Asiatic missions, sixty thousand passed over the line that parts idolatrous and Christian communities; and twenty persons in Christian lands gave to foreign missions about four millions of dollars, — two developments that have had no parallel in history.

No human wisdom can forecast the possible revelations of even the immediate future. So rapid and so radical are the changes taking place, that before these pages can get into print, what is written will have ceased to be accurate. Even as we write, new issues of the missionary magazines have come into our hands, compelling revision of what is not yet stereotyped into permanence! These grand bulletin boards of missions are full of news. New Zealand has an army of twelve thousand teetotalers; the island of Hainan in China clamors for Christian schools, and is wide open to the gospel. Dr. McKay, at Formosa, who when he went there found idolatry rampant, the people bitter toward foreigners, and without preachers, churches, or hospitals — recently, at his fourteenth anniversary, welcomed thirteen hundred converts who gathered at Tamsiu to express their grateful love; and since then, in ten days he has baptized over twelve hundred more! The Society for the Propagation of the Gospel in Foreign Parts reports over two thousand baptisms in the Madras district during 1885. And these are but a few of the stirring reports that from all quarters announce new doors opening, new fields inviting, new demands urging, new successes cheering. Verily it is the crisis of missions, and there is a voice out of the cloud, "Go FORWARD!"

CHAPTER XXVIII.

THE ELEMENTS IN THE CRISIS.

THE main purpose of the preceding pages is to impress the great fact that we have reached the most critical point in missionary history.

What is a crisis? It is a combination of grand opportunity and great responsibility; the hour when the chance of glorious success and the risk of awful failure confront each other; the turning-point of history and destiny. We do not say the crisis of missions *is coming*, — it *has come*, and is even now upon us. There have been repeated crises before, but THE CRISIS is now to be met. Never, since Christ committed a world's evangelization to His servants, have such open doors of opportunity, such providential removal of barriers and subsidence of obstacles, such general preparation for the universal and immediate dissemination of the gospel, and such triumphs of grace in the work of missions, supplied such inspiration to angelic zeal and seraphic devotion; but it may well be doubted whether there has ever been greater risk of losing the opportunity. We are in peril of practical apathy, if not apostasy, with respect to this stewardship of the gospel, this obligation to a lost world.

We have looked upon the fruitful, hopeful mission field, with its providential leadings and gracious workings; but to the brightest picture there is often a darker background; and it is necessary to a complete impression, that we should candidly face all the facts, however they may rebuke our listlessness and selfishness. And a few of these discouragements we must carefully and prayerfully consider, if we would understand and solve the problem of missions.

First of all, the Church is moving so slowly that Satan's active agents are entering these open doors, preoccupying these open fields.

The crisis will not brook delay. Satan appreciates his opportunity, if we do not ours. If we do not push our forces to the front, we shall find it too late. We can take possession, then, if at all, only by dislodging a foe whom our delays have permitted to precede us.

India is an example of the danger of delay. The theosophists go there and feed the expiring flame of paganism with the fuel of rationalism and mysticism. In Calcutta, Paine's "Age of Reason" is made "plain upon the tablets," instead of the gospel; and in university cities like Bombay, natives eagerly read and glibly quote Hegel, Strauss, Renan, and Ingersoll, like the blatant sceptics of young America. European books and teachers import materialism and atheism, sugar-coated with subtle science and seductive philosophy. The "Liberal Christians" send out a solitary missionary to convert the East Indians to Unitarianism, and he himself becomes a convert to the famous Brahmo Somaj, showing that a nominal and Christless gospel is more likely to be vanquished than victorious in conflict with paganism.

Japan, again, warns us of the risk of procrastination in missions. A nation ready to be moulded is liable to be marred; the pliant sapling may be easily deformed, or the plastic clay shaped for dishonor. Into these openings go the devil's agents, if the Lord's do not; and while we sleep they sow tares in the mellow soil. What can be more important than, at the crisis of Japan's history and destiny, to flood the land with the gospel! A whole people, forsaking the effete faith of their forefathers, asks for a better. Such another day will never again come for that land, and the door cannot long stand open. It is now or never!

Shintooism may be powerless and Buddhism be in its decadence, and the priests confess the downfall of the old faiths; but the philosophies of the pantheist and materialist, atheist and agnostic, are even now boldly taught. Spencer, Huxley, Darwin and Buckle, Mill and Strauss, diffuse their new gospel, and education is linking itself with infidelity. Meanwhile, nominal Christianity with its ceremonialism, the form of godliness without its power, comes to entrench itself. Romanism, expelled in the seventeenth century, jesuitically renews its efforts to convert the Japanese in the nineteenth.

In papal lands, again, delay is irreparable damage. The popular current is away from Rome, but in the direction of infidelity. Millions are sick of priest-craft, and feel clericalism to be the foe of freedom and well-being. But the reaction is toward no religion; in breaking away from the bonds of superstition there is a proneness to refuse all restraints of conscience and divine law.

These multitudes are grossly ignorant, to a degree of which we have little conception. The little ones in our Protestant Sunday-schools at least know the Bible from the prayer-book, which many a Romanist does not. So, in the Greek Church, a Russian peasant thought the Trinity was composed of " the Saviour, the Mother of God, and St.

Nicholas, the miracle-worker." Thousands of adherents of these churches have absolutely no knowledge of evangelical truth. Their ignorance leaves them at the mercy of designing demagogues, corrupt politicians, and infidel anarchists. They need enlightenment; and as ignorance gives way to intelligence, the intellect that is casting off its shackles must, by a coeducation of intellect and conscience, be kept from running liberty into license. Now is the time, when eyes are opening, to pour in the light of the gospel.

Once more, we seem to see the angel standing with one foot upon the sea and the other upon the land, with the open book in his hand, and to hear him swear that "there shall be *delay no longer;* "[1] while to God's Church comes His majestic message, " Thou must prophesy again before many peoples and nations and tongues and kings."

There can be neither excuse nor extenuation for the sluggishness that leaves the emissaries of the devil to preoccupy the mission

[1] Rev. x. 6, margin.

field, and sow the tares before we have sown the seed of the kingdom; to furnish the pagan with a coat of mail wherewith to ward off the arrows of the truth. While the missionary press, suffering from financial drought, sends its little rill of pure water into desert places, Satan's presses, with royal riches at disposal, flood the land with poisoned streams of Western scepticism. It is the old parable illustrated. Here is the house of heathenism, out of which has gone the unclean spirit; but we leave it empty, and seven other spirits more wicked than the first enter in and dwell there; and the last state is worse than the first. Oh for the zeal that pushes into the house in advance of the evil one!

There is no discouragement that need dismay a living, praying, working church. John, in apocalyptic vision, and as the final victory of the hosts of God draws nigh, sees the " devil come down, having great wrath, because he knoweth that he hath but a short time." The violence of Satan makes no impression on a well panoplied church, whose shield of faith is able to quench even his fiery darts; but to a church lacking in missionary principle and activity he may work disaster that centuries will not repair.

Every conceivable motive, therefore, urges us to undertake the last great crusade against the powers of darkness. The command of our ascended Lord, the voice of an enlightened conscience, the impulse of the new nature, the leading of the providential pillar, the working of transforming grace, the grandeur of the opportunity and the peril of delay, — all these converge like rays in one burning focus, urging us onward and forward to the outposts of civilization and the limits of human habitation with the word of life. Let the trumpet signal be heard all along the lines! God has already sounded His signal, and, like that peal at Sinai, it is long and loud. The last precept and promise of our Lord, which have inspired all true service and sacrifice, echo with new force and emphasis, louder and clearer, in the face of new openings and new victories. Blessed is he who, like Paul, is immediately obedient unto the heavenly vision.

CHAPTER XXIX.

 SECOND important element in the crisis of missions is the practical insensibility and indifference of the Church as a whole.

Dr. Anderson, whose words have been already quoted, said, with painful conviction, that the greatest lack of the church of our day is that it does not yield a ready response to the providence of God. God's voice is heard, awful with divine majesty, imperial in its authority, commanding an advance of the entire host and a combined assault upon the citadels of the enemy; and while the voice speaks the cloud moves, leading the way, marking its course by constant conquest, inspiring obedient souls with courage, and assuring those who have the faith and fortitude to follow, that complete triumph is before them.

Yet, while every motive urges and impels us forward, we are in some respects going backward.   Unbelief, instead of echoing God's call for enlargement, actually dares to cry, " Retrenchment! "   That has been the motto of our mission boards for ten years; it has echoed through our mission fields like a death-knell to missionary advance.   Last year in one of our important mission centres in Asia the only boys' school, girls' seminary, and printing-press had to be closed for want of money to carry them on.   A great Board, oppressed with debt, and vainly appealing to the churches for help, said to its representatives abroad, " You must cut down your outlay at least one tenth."   And so at a time when even to stand still is to fall back, this cry of " Retrench! " became the keynote of missions.

The gospel is God's economy of grace for the entire race of man, sunk in the same ruin.

By the first Adam came one generic fall, and by the second Adam comes one generic redemption, — a universal remedy for universal sin. Between these lost souls and this great salvation, the one living link is the believer, whose lips and whose life are to unite in witnessing to the "Lamb of God who taketh away the sin of the world." The glorious work, the dispensation of the gospel, is committed to us all; being one with Christ by faith, love and labor are to make us a bond between Him and the lost whom He came to seek and to save.

Here is an "altar that sanctifies the gift." The widow's mites, laid thereon, are not only sanctified, but magnified and glorified: they grow into shekels of the sanctuary, precious as gold, pellucid as crystal. But when, better than the richest offerings, *self* is laid on the altar of missions, God's own fire comes down, not to consume but to consecrate and glorify. Our Lord waits to "see of the travail of His soul," and to "be satisfied;" and the sluggishness, selfishness, and, shall we say it? stinginess, of disciples actually hinder the great consummation!

We shall have to account, as a Church, for an apathy that verges on apostasy. We should forget the trifles that often engross our thoughts and even our meetings as churches and as courts of Christ; cease to contend over mere secular issues, points of order, clerical etiquette, and minor matters of all sorts; and send forth through the Church one mighty clarion-call, in God's name demanding both consecrated capital and consecrated character, to fill the needs of our mission fields. In such an hour as this not even prayer will suffice. For nearly a century the church of God has been lying on her face before God, asking for an open path through impassable barriers. Between us and the thousand million pagans a Red Sea lay, too broad to bridge, too deep to wade, too angry and stormy to cross. God has driven it back, and here is a dry highway: the waters that were a wall to obstruct are now a wall to protect. What are we still lying on our

face for, praying for God's interposition?
He says, "Wherefore criest thou unto me?
Go forward!" This is not a time to stop,
even to pray. We must not delay. Just
now, "*laborare est orare*," — work is worship.
Yes, work is worship; what James calls the
δεησις ενεργουμενη — the energetic supplication — is just now the only acceptable prayer.
There are times when the only true supplication is the supply of men and means and material of war. The Church has been asking for
nearly two thousand years that the kingdoms
of this world might become the kingdom of
our Lord and of His Christ. And now, behold
the highway for our God! mountains levelled,
valleys exalted, to make a plain, level road
from Christendom as a centre, to the ends of
the earth. The chariot of God is ready; but
notwithstanding it has a divine motor, it
moves very slowly, because the stones are
not gathered out of the way, and professed
disciples drag on it as a dead weight. Avarice, appetite, ambition, a secular spirit, engrossing worldly schemes, ignorance of facts,

and practical indifference, block the way; while lazy self-indulgence, enervating luxury, vicious habits of selfishness, forgetfulness of stewardship, leave the very church of God to hang as a hinderance upon the wheels, instead of pushing them onward. Vain to pray that "the Word of the Lord may have free course and be glorified," while such hinderances are encouraged.

There is little danger of exaggerating the grandeur of our opportunity, or the greatness of our responsibility, or the peril of unfaithfulness, neglect, or even delay. The church of God must answer to the Master for the practical indifference that to-day curses our membership in the matter of missions. A whole generation is going down to the grave. What we are going to do for our fellow-men of our generation must be done while they remain to be reached, and we remain to reach them.

Does the Church appreciate the privilege of being co-workers together with God? There is a definite purpose in His mind, and

He has been working along the lines of that plan, steadily, from the beginning. That plan is bound to succeed. Even our apathy cannot thwart it. But He may be compelled to do with us as He did with the Oriental churches of the apostolic age, that, engrossed in selfishness, wrapped themselves in Laodicean self-complacency and were spued out of His mouth like lukewarm water. Our candlestick will be removed out of its place if we do not hold forth the Word of life, and shine as lights in the world; and another church will take the place of the church of this generation that refuses to respond to the Providence of God and obey the signals from the great Commander.

The Earl of Cairns, in his last missionary appeal before the Church Missionary Society, in Exeter Hall, March 24, 1885, urged on his hearers the great considerations not of duty so much as of privilege. In this work we enter into partnership with God. Every dollar given to missions, and every effort or prayer put forth in their behalf, are expressions of fellowship in God's eternal purpose and work; and this is why the altar so sanctifies the gift. He told a short but simple story illustrating this. In Belfast there was a little boy, a chimney-sweep. He happened to be attracted by missions, and contributed to a mission-box a sum which was not inconsiderable for a chimney-sweep, — the sum of twopence. One afternoon a friend of this boy met him going along the street in an unusual condition, for his hands and his face were washed, and he was dressed in very good clothes. And the friend said to him, "Halloa! where are you going?" "Oh," he said, "I am going to a missionary meeting." — "What are you going to a missionary meeting for?" "Well," said the sweep, "you see I have become a sort of partner in the concern, and I am going to see how the business is getting on."

It is even so. He who in any way hearing the call, responds to it with prayers and tears, with service and sacrifice, with the gifts of wealth or the mites of poverty, with labor or with life, is a partner with God in the celestial business of bringing salvation to a lost world; and no man, woman, or child can give prayerfully without a growing intensity of interest, watching how the business is getting on.

Thomas Cooper[1] has told us that Handel's Hallelujah Chorus was an inspiration. This grandest of all musical harmonies was composed to celebrate the spread of the Redeemer's kingdom. " The Bible and all it reveals — but more especially the theme of redemption — dwelt much in Handel's memory and in his heart and mind. He grasped the statements of Christianity as facts, — facts as remarkable as his own existence; and rejoiced with an elevated joy in the belief that this Christianity would one day fill the earth. It is this elevated joy of his own heart and soul that he strives to express in his unequalled Hallelujah."

Lord Northbrook, at the Church Missionary meeting in June, referred to his feelings

---

[1] Thoughts at Fourscore, p. 345.

at hearing this glorious chorus sung at the opening of the Indian and Colonial Exhibition, adding, that it was not so much the music as the words and thoughts that thrilled him. This greatest of all musical creations was inspired by the faith that from sea to sea, and from the river to the ends of the earth, His dominion shall extend; and that from every part of this earth shall yet rise the choral shout, " Hallelujah! for the Lord God omnipotent reigneth." Even so, Lord Jesus, come quickly!

That is the grander chorus, of which Handel's Hallelujah is but the faint and distant anticipation. It will combine the voices of patriarchs and prophets, apostles and martyrs, and all loyal, loving saints of all the ages. Nor is there in all the world, in the obscurest hovel of poverty, one humble soul that prays "Thy kingdom come," that lays consecrated offerings on the altar of missions, who shall not join that final anthem, as one who has helped forward the great consummation.

CHAPTER XXX.

A THIRD element in this crisis demands a special notice, for it may, in part, account for the shameful apathy and lethargy that allow a thousand millions of human beings to live and die without the gospel. We refer to the practical doubt, if not denial, of their lost condition, which is largely the fruit of the attempt to improve upon the old gospel.

A subtle leaven is pervading the lump. Evangelistic effort was almost abandoned for a thousand years through the loss of the sense of obligation and responsibility. During the Dark Ages there was no missionary activity. Even after the great Reformation had dawned in Wycliffe, and Savonarola, Huss, Luther, Knox, and Calvin had borne the fiery cross into Italy, Bohemia, Germany, Scotland, and Switzerland, it took three centuries to bring the Reformed Churches to see that " the field is the world," and " that the good seed are the children of the kingdom," who are not only to sow the Word of God in the soil of every part of that field, but to plant themselves as living witnesses in the midst of pagan society, and become, even from martyr-graves, the seed of a harvest of souls!

The duty of a world-wide evangelism is now universally recognized, or at least not denied. Even churches that do nothing and give nothing have not the temerity to dispute the claims of a lost world upon those who have the " corn," and will get a curse if they " withhold it." But now another " paralytic stroke " dulls our nerves of sensation and palsies our nerves of motion. There is a current, though unexpressed, belief that a universal and saving element runs through all religious systems; that there is a " Light of Asia " as well as a " Light of the world; "

that Christianity is only an evolutional product, the tenth and best of all the " religions,"
and the fittest to survive, but not the only
faith that contains elevating, and even redeeming, influences.

" God is not so unjust," it is said, " as to allow the heathen, who never heard of Christ,
to perish because they were not converted ; "
and so the responsibility of conveying to them
the message of salvation is thrown off without
much disturbance of conscience.   In fact, an
intelligent man once evaded an earnest appeal
in behalf of the heathen by declaring it " pre-
sumptuous to interfere with other people in
the peaceable enjoyment of their religion."

This apathy of misconception, this paral-
ysis of action, are encouraged, and we are
lulled to a death-like torpor and stupor, by
the " new theology."   There is a wide-spread
hope of a probation after death, of a restoration of the wicked after a purgatorial punish-
ment, or of a final restitution of all things,
when even Moab and Edom, Tyre and Phil-
istia, are to take their place among the

nations, and have an opportunity to embrace Immanuel as Saviour and King.

This is the Devil's master-piece of strategy to keep the hosts of God within the walls of luxurious indolence, when they should march and move outward against the citadels of superstition and idolatry. The old heresies, scotched but not killed, revive from stunning and seemingly fatal blows, to renew the conflict upon modern fields. Paul encountered those in his day who opposed evangelistic labor, " forbidding us to speak to the Gentiles that they might be saved, to fill up their sins alway; for the wrath is come upon them to the uttermost."[1]

We must either give up the inspiration of the Word, or accept the lost condition of the world. The epistle to the Romans leaves no standing-room for candid doubt, unless we deny that Paul spake under the moving of the Holy Ghost. That masterly epistle, which is logic on fire, begins with a fearful indictment of the whole pagan world for idolatry

[1] 1 Thess. ii. 16.

and iniquity; and affirms that "they are *without excuse*, because that when they knew God, they glorified Him not as God," etc.

The speculative question as to the spiritual estate and prospects of the heathen is here answered practically. They are not condemned for rejecting Christ whom they had no opportunity to accept, nor for not using light which they did not have; but because they shut their eyes to the light which they had, "did not like to retain God in their knowledge," and "*held down* the truth in unrighteousness," as a man holds down and chokes an antagonist. In every age the heathen have had more knowledge of God than they have desired or used. Ever since creation there have been open before men the book of nature, manifesting His eternal power and Godhood; and the book of their own complex nature, with its divine powers of thought, love, conscience, and will. From these, as well as from God's providence in history, they might have read of Him. Yet they perversely deified blocks of wood and stone, and worshipped the created thing — from the sun down to the beetle — rather than the Creator. They ran from the light to their dark holes, like bugs that burrow in the earth; they abandoned themselves to crime, lust, sin; and so God judicially abandoned them, first to uncleanness, then to vile affections, and last of all to a reprobate mind. They are to be judged not by our supernatural light, but by their own natural light; they sinned without law, and without law they perish.

This argument in the first chapter Paul supplements in the tenth by a series of questions. "How then shall they call on him in whom they have not believed? and how shall they believe in him of whom they have not heard? and how shall they hear without a preacher? and how shall they preach except they be sent?" These questions are indirect affirmations that the preacher must be sent to them, that they may hear, and hearing, believe, and believing, call, and calling, be saved.

This does not limit the power or grace of God. If there be anywhere a soul feeling after God, following the light of nature and of conscience, in hope and faith that the Great Unknown will somehow give more light, and lead to life and blessedness, we may safely leave such to His fatherly care. He who sent Peter to tell a Roman centurion words whereby he and his house might be saved; He who went to the very coasts of Canaan, to help one poor woman; He who bade Philip join the Ethiopian eunuch, that he might guide a perplexed inquirer, — will not leave any sincere seeker to seek in vain.

But this concession does not touch the practical question of a world's degradation and destitution. If there come up, to those twelve gates that open to every quarter, a Confucius, a Zoroaster, a Socrates, a Seneca, a Buddha, or some who from huts and hovels looked for a dawn that never greeted and gladdened their eyes, God may so glorify His grace, and demonstrate the possibility of any real inquirer's being led and lifted up by

God; but the salvation of the few would only justify the condemnation of the rest.

It is time disciples were done with spiritual Darwinism. The religion of Christ is no evolution from other faiths, and survival of the fittest. Like Aaron's rod, it swallows all the others, embracing all that is true in any other faith; but, like Aaron's rod, it is the only rod that buds, for it alone is the power and wisdom of God unto salvation. If life is to come to the dead, it must be by the touch of this divine rod. We are not left to the capricious winds of human doctrine, and the sleight and cunning craftiness of men who lie in wait to deceive. The Word of God is our only guide and authority, and it gives no uncertain sound. We hear there not one word about salvation without Christ. All are concluded under sin, and involved in one condemnation; to all alike one gospel is sent, and must be borne by those who have it.

God counts silence, inaction, indifference among mortal sins. The blood of a thousand millions of souls will be required of this generation.   Nearly two thousand years have gone by since our Lord said, " Go ye into all the world and preach the gospel to every creature ; " and yet Christendom stands idly facing a lost world, grudgingly sends ten thousand workers into the world-field, and gives ten millions of dollars a year for the work ; and then lazily swings in silken hammocks spun out of fine theories and speculations about " second probation " and " final restoration ; " sinks into calm repose, surfeited with repasts whose crumbs would feed a starving world ; and at last ventures into the presence of God, to face a whole generation of lost souls for whose salvation no personal effort has practically been made !

When the Holy Ghost endues us for service, He first anoints our eyes with eye-salve, that we may see the hell of hopelessness into which souls are sinking.   Only when we see and feel this to be the fact shall we be divinely impelled and compelled to shout the tidings of salvation, till it sounds in the sepulchres of heathendom like the trump of God.

CHAPTER XXXI.

THE SPIRIT OF MISSIONS.

IN such a crisis as this there is but one thing that can be done to meet the emergency. Those within the church who feel its importance, who accept as a fact the ruin of a lost race, and who respond to the providence of God, must, without waiting for any new conditions in the church at large, move forward in faith and prayer, relying upon Him who can enable one to chase a thousand, and two to put ten thousand to flight; with Whom all things are possible.

There is too much work yet to be done to allow of delay. We cannot even wait for reinforcements. Hundreds of millions of human beings have not yet heard so much as the faintest echo of the gospel trumpet.

Mission stations, even where most thickly planted, are but scattered oases in an immense stretch of desert, or stars in a firmament,— centres of vast vacancies. Contrasted with the hosts of unsaved, untaught heathen, all missionary laborers together form but an insignificant number. Among the more cultivated and among the more degraded pagans, only a bare start has been made toward evangelization; the territory of Islam is yet almost intact; and even where missions have been most successful, the extent of the dominion of the death-shade is so great, that millions often constitute the parish dependent upon one man's curacy.

Every day's delay complicates the problem. While we are sounding the silver trumpets to rally a sluggish host to the onset, the emissaries of infidelity preoccupy the field. A vicious education rears new barriers between pagan hearts and the gospel. And so in many ways the professed disciples of Christ are not only failing in their duty to this lost world, but are responsible for permitting new obstacles to accumulate. With a sad heart we record the deep conviction that in the lack of the spirit of missions within the church itself lies both the secret of the slow response to our Lord's appeal, and the main hinderance to the world's evangelization.

In not a few cases the *principle* of missions is not practically operative in our church life. Some of God's people have not yet learned the lesson that the conditions of vitality in a church are not only self-government and self-support, but self-propagation. The seed that sprang up among thorns grew long and spindling, but it all ran to stalk; there were no kernels in the ear. What a picture of the Christians in whom the cares of the world, the deceitfulness of riches, and the lusts of other things entering in choke the word, so that, whatever be the apparent growth and outward prosperity, there is developed no full-grown corn in the ear, no seed of propagation by which other harvest fields are to be sown! Hundreds of evangelical congregations give nothing to missions at home or abroad, and the blanks in the columns of reports year by year seem to cause them no blushes of shame. Sheldon Dibble's remark, as to the need of Christians to be converted to an interest in missions, finds an echo in Christlieb's declaration of the need of a threefold conversion: namely, of the *heart*, to secure holy affections; of the *head*, to assure right convictions; and of the *purse*, to assure ample offerings.

Where this principle of missions is not firmly rooted and practically fruitful, not only does it hinder missions, but the Church runs risk in breathing its own atmosphere. Dr. Duff has observed that the church that is no longer evangelistic will soon cease to be evangelical. The weapons of aggressive warfare are the best protection for defensive warfare. Missions are the best apologetics, for they are the dynamics of the Church, the vindication and justification of our faith, the sure means of strength and growth; and to enshrine and enthrone missions in the very heart of the Church is the surest hope of a revival of pure and primitive piety at home.

That missions should need a plea in their behalf marks the low ebb of spiritual life. The very nature of the word of life is to run and spread. " You cannot gather water in heaps, unless you allow it to freeze." Fire will spread while it finds fuel, and when it can no longer spread, dies away, first to embers and then to ashes. The plea of inability to give is often not only selfish, but hypocritical. Even in a financial crisis plenty of money is found for luxury and frivolity. Such selfishness is, we fear, the cloak of an unregenerate heart. A personal faith in Christ begets a personal love for the lost, whom He came to seek and to save; and, as Christlieb phrases it, " He who cannot stand on this platform is the object of missions, not the subject of them." We do not need Max Müller to tell us that " Christianity is in its nature a missionary religion, converting, advancing, aggressive, encompassing the world," so long as the divine key-note of all church history and church life has been struck in the command of Christ himself: " Go ye into all the world and preach the gospel to every creature." A church cold toward missions will find heathenism in popular forms gaining ground within her courts, till the theological theses of her candidates for licensure betray a destructive scepticism, like some in Bonn, which assaulted belief in the miraculous as an " epidemic insanity."

The principle of missions is not enough, however, without the *spirit* of missions; a law of labor for souls will not suffice without the love for Christ and for souls, which is the life-secret of such labor. While the spirit of missions is still lacking, no machinery will be adequate; the men and money will still be shamefully inadequate, both to the extent of the field and the needs of the work, and to the number of disciples and the means at their disposal. Give us the spirit of missions, and the territory now scarcely approached will be at once surrounded, penetrated, possessed; and a new motive-power will be supplied, that will transform cold duty into ecstatic delight.

Only this spirit of missions can ever supply the deficiency of laborers. The fields of the papacy, now so strangely opening to the circulation of the Bible and the preaching of the cross, inviting the sowing of the seed of the kingdom, and yielding harvests so rapidly that reaper overtakes ploughman, — these fields alone might well occupy all the laborers now at work throughout the whole mission field. At this very day the working force should be multiplied fifty-fold in Syria, Persia, and Korea; a hundred-fold in India, Turkey, and Japan; and a thousand-fold in China, Africa, and the papal states.

We need the spirit of missions to increase our gifts. There is quite as much deficiency in money as in men; our gifts to the great cause are alarmingly disproportionate both to the openings for work and to our ability. From the four quarters the very wings of the wind waft to our ears the Macedonian cry;

and yet our missionary boards bow, year after year, under a load of debt, which, if lifted by herculean effort, is only renewed. And in the midst of a work which will not bear even to stand still, we are actually going back. God bore much from Israel's unbelief in the desert. Is He bearing nothing from His church of to-day?

We should cherish not only the principle and the spirit of missions, but also secure thorough organization and co-operation. No congregation is so small or weak that it needs, or can afford, to pass missions by. The weakness, assigned as a cause, is often a consequence of such neglect. It keeps a church weak to do nothing for those who are without; unselfish effort quickens its pulse and strengthens its sinews. Self-extension reacts to promote self-support; and if churches now having only a name to live would nourish and cherish the spirit of missions, there would be growth both in numbers and in graces. The Moravians, with but twenty thousand adult communicants, have no rival as a missionary body. One out of every seventy of their membership is in the mission field; and out of their poverty they raise an annual missionary income of $240,-000, an average of twelve dollars per member! Even the smallest and the poorest disciple is expected to give something to further the Lord's work.

A thorough organization for the work will include a thorough dissemination of a cheap, attractive missionary literature. The facts must be more widely known. We must put new life into our concerts for prayer. Our whole church activity must be consecrated by a new spirit; otherwise, even in the midst of a bustling activity, we may incur what Warneck counts the chief risk, "that missionary enterprise shall glide into mere routine, missionary zeal become so much rhetoric, and participation in missionary work degenerate into mere habit, not to say ecclesiastical business."

We need a more consecrated ministry. Here the revival of the missionary spirit must begin. "Like people, like priest." (The pastor's life usually fixes the flood-mark for the tides of church life, and very seldom do they rise higher.) William Burns incarnated the gospel; and to this day the Chinese feel the power of his consecration. When pastors burn and glow with a divine ardor and fervor toward the work of universal missions, the people will raise a loftier standard of missionary zeal. Dr. Duff, when leaving for India in 1829, said: "There was a time when I had no care or concern for the heathen; that was when I had none for my own soul. When by the grace of God I was led to care for my own soul, I began to care for them. In my closet I said: 'O Lord, silver and gold have I none. What I have I give: I offer Thee myself! Wilt Thou accept the gift?'"

We need a more hallowed and missionary atmosphere in our colleges and seminaries. There it is that the ministers are made; and there the first battles of the missionary field are fought, as Waterloo was fought at Eton.

The question of duty to the heathen presents itself during the preparation for the sacred calling. How much depends on the careful, prayerful weighing of these august claims! He who is not ready for a life of self-denial hastily dismisses them; carnal considerations give the casting vote in favor of home fields that promise richer returns of salary, human praise, worldly promotion, and personal ease. We need spiritually minded men in the chairs of our educational institutions, who shall plainly teach, as Professor Phelps sharply puts it, that he who is not ready to preach the gospel anywhere, is fit to preach it nowhere.

CHAPTER XXXII.

THE LIVING LINKS.

ONE of the practical difficulties in the way of the prosecution of missions is found in the immensity of the field, and its remoteness. Even the most diligent student of missions finds that his knowledge only makes him more conscious of his ignorance; and the money given seems like a little water scattered over vast territories cursed with perpetual drought. As to the great mass of our church members, they know nothing about the subject, and have only a vague notion that about a thousand million of souls are in darkness and destitution. Their offerings are put into a bag with holes: they drop out of sight, and fall somewhere, but are never traced, or heard from again. How it would quicken both praying and giving, if there could be a little closer contact between the Church and the awful destitution of heathendom!

A great lack in our churches is the lack of *living links* between them and the foreign field. When one of their own number goes abroad, and is supported by the church at home; where contributions to the support of teachers, schools, or pupils abroad bring back letters of a personal character; where, in any way, direct communication and contact are established by correspondence with a definite field, — it is very helpful in the increase both of knowledge and of zeal. The highest ideal of beneficence is that in which our gifts are guided by that sublimely unselfish spirit that embraces the whole world, and is content to pour liberally into the missionary treasury without tracing the streams to their terminus. But we are all weak saints. It is well to be disinterested; but the danger just now is of being *un*interested. The Church has been classified into " Mission, Anti-Mission, and Omission " Christians, and nothing practically reduces the latter two classes more than direct relations with some field through some known and loved missionary. The church that sends out laborers from its own number, and through them becomes acquainted with the field, its people, wants, discouragements, and developments, will grow in intelligence, sympathy, offerings, and prayers for the whole work. We are deeply persuaded that such living links between the home churches and the mission field are means of grace. After long watching of the development of the missionary spirit in active, aggressive churches, we have come to the calm conclusion that if this great work is to be properly prosecuted, each church must have some definite field to work, and must send to and support in that field its own workers.

This need not interfere with the general prosecution of missions, by leaving obscure and unattractive fields to be neglected. Let the assignment of the separate fields be left to the missionary boards, as the channels of distribution and communication; let there be a general offering for the general work, as well as special offerings for particular workers in chosen fields. But let us have in our church life the incentive, the inspiration, found in the closer study of some one people with their customs, creeds, religions; some one field with its needs and claims; and let the men and women, sent out from our own church-home, both draw out our interest, sympathy, prayers, and gifts toward the field, and be the channel of information and intelligence from the field to us.

Pastor Harms's church in Hermansburgh is the convincing proof and illustration of this law of human nature. In 1849, thirty-seven years ago, a glimpse of the destitution of heathendom, as they saw it through the eyes of a poor, disabled candidate, moved that congregation of poor peasants, farmers, and laborers, to organize a society for sending the gospel to foreign parts. A widow brought six shillings, a laborer sixpence, and a child a silver penny. And upon this slender pecuniary basis was built up the most colossal individual missionary enterprise of the ages. No bolder act is to be found in the history of missions than that of Louis Harms, when he proposed to his people to be their own missionaries, when he undertook to inspire poor farmers, ignorant peasants, and rude day-laborers to volunteer for missionary purposes, and both create and sustain, alike with money and men, their own missions. It was very decidedly "out of the usual course," and so was the first Pentecost; but, like that, it was a moving of God. All the zeal of that parish was turned into a new channel, and the first definite development was the coming forward of volunteers who offered to become the living links between Hermansburgh in Hanover and heathendom. One volunteer brought his farm, and this, with its plain farm-house, was turned into a training-school.

Africa was chosen as a field, and the training of the raw recruits began. A sailor who joined the ranks suggested the building of the ship, and in 1853 the "Candace" sailed with a missionary colony comprising eight missionaries, two smiths, a tailor, butcher, dyer, and three laborers. They sought to pierce through Natal among the Kaffirs, and work north, linking station to station in a chain. They were in constant exchange of missionary intelligence and friendly personal letters; and in order to diffuse this intelligence more widely, and develop these personal ties of sympathy more richly, a missionary magazine was established, edited and published on the premises of their own training-school. That ship moving to and fro was the shuttle weaving a closer and fuller bond of contact with heathen peoples, and those letters and gifts and living men and women were the fleshly fibres woven and braided into that bond. That ship was a constant appeal and challenge; and as often as it returned, new recruits were ready. More than forty left at one time, and in one year, 1863, one hundred offered themselves.

During the seventeen years of Louis Harms's conduct of the enterprise, that parish enjoyed one long revival, and ten thousand members were gathered into that church-fold; while the work grew abroad, so that in 1883, thirty years after the "Candace" first set sail, over thirty stations had been established, they had forty ordained missionaries, fifty-five lay, and as many more women, missionaries, twenty-two natives ordained, and one hundred and eighty-five helpers, — a total working force of three hundred and fifty-seven; had gathered three thousand nine hundred and twenty communicants, and eight thousand five hundred and twenty adherents, from heathendom, and spent that year seventy thousand five hundred dollars. Instead of finding their sympathies and efforts narrowing by such specific labors in one field, the result has been to expand and enrich their missionary spirit, to render it more catholic and cosmopolitan; and so we find them sending missionaries to India, Australia, and even America.

Let it be observed that this small and obscure parish in Hanover had no proxies or substitutes. They constituted their own board, became their own secretaries, edited their own missionary magazine, and organized and administered their own mission work. Is it not barely possible that the boards of foreign missions, instead of being the mere agents or instruments of the active benevolence of our churches, are in too many cases a substitute for it? Are not our people quite too content to give an annual offering to missions through some such treasury, leaving to wise and able secretaries not only to distribute funds and workers, but to conduct all correspondence? When intelligence from the field is printed in a missionary magazine, only some twenty thousand copies of it are circulated among hundreds of thousands of communicants, and out of that twenty thousand, one-quarter sent gratuitously to ministers and missionaries. Would it not be a grand help to the diffusion of missionary intelligence, to the

increase of missionary offerings, and to
the awakening of a profoundly prayerful,
personal, and sympathetic interest, if each
church might be linked to the heathen
world by the life of some consecrated man
or woman; and best of all, if that person be
one sent out from among their own number,
known personally, loved dearly, whose very
name becomes inseparably connected with
the work of a world's redemption? If the
life of Harriet Newell, Adoniram Judson,
David Livingstone, Alexander Duff, makes
all our pulses bound anew with yearnings
to save the lost, what would be the effect
on any church from which such heroic souls
went down into the deep mine of heathenism,
charging those whom they left behind to hold
the rope?

The experiment is surely worth the trial.
After centuries of comparative failure to compass this great want, we may well undertake
some new scheme, such as in so many in-
stances has proven grandly successful in culti-
vating the spirit of missions. If nothing more

is feasible, surely certain missionary laborers might be put in correspondence with particular churches, whose offerings might be appropriated for their support, wholly or partially. What is desirable is that the churches at home, and the mission fields and mission workers abroad, should get into contact and communication; so that the bond of sympathy, conscious fellowship, and intelligent interest might grow and become more vital; so that the same influences which now reach so powerfully the hearts of our devoted missionary secretaries might thrill and vitalize the dead body of our church membership. Where is the church that supports a missionary in a foreign field, and gets soul-stirring letters from such a missionary, that does not feel more interest in all the fields and all the workers?

CHAPTER XXXIII.

THE PROBLEM OF MISSIONS.

HE spirit of missions being cherished, and developed by a true organization, the great problem, requiring a solution, is the lack of men and of means to occupy the field and to accomplish the work.

We may roughly estimate the souls that in Pagan, Moslem, Papal, and nominally Christian lands still need to be reached with a pure gospel at a thousand millions; and the whole number of missionary laborers, at thirty-five thousand. Could each of these carry on the work of evangelization, independently, each worker would have to care for nearly thirty thousand souls. As a matter of fact, more than twenty-five thousand of these laborers are unordained native assistants, fit only to aid trained workmen; so that we have not more than ten thousand missionaries, native and foreign, competent to conduct this work. Each of these must therefore assume an *average responsibility of one hundred thousand souls ;* meanwhile, the total sum annually spent on foreign missions is about *ten millions of dollars,* — an allowance of *one cent a year for each soul of this thousand million !*

Nothing can be plainer, without argument, than that the church of Christ has never yet attempted to solve the problem of missions. Dr. Duff was right in saying that we are "playing at missions." Were true, sound, sensible business principles applied to this question, no practical hinderance would be found sufficient even to delay the prosecution of the work solemnly committed by Christ to His church. Let us have throughout the Church thorough organization and practical co-operation, and within the lifetime of one generation the gospel may be preached for a witness, not only among all nations, but to every living creature.

Let us consider that here is the command of the King of kings, for more than eighteen centuries waiting for obedient disciples to carry it out. Mordecai, five hundred years before Christ, issued a decree in the name of Ahasuerus. It was the third month, Sivan, on the three and twentieth day, that the king's scribes were called to put that decree in writing; it was addressed to the Jews, lieutenants, deputies, and rulers of the provinces which reached from India unto Ethiopia,—a hundred and twenty-seven provinces; it had to be translated into the language of each province, and promulgated with haste. There were no facilities for doing this work such as we possess; no printing-presses, postal unions, telegraphs; no railroads and steam-ships. Every copy must be transcribed by hand, and the messengers must go only so fast as horses and mules, camels and dromedaries, could carry them. And yet through all those hundred and twenty-seven provinces the decree was published upon the thirteenth day of the twelfth month,

Adar. *Less than nine months* to bear the king's message throughout his wide domain, while the church of Christ, after nearly *nineteen hundred years*, has reached only *one fourth of the human race* with the gospel of salvation.

An English preacher asked some British soldiers, " If Queen Victoria were to issue a proclamation, and, placing it in the hands of her army and navy, were to say, ' Go ye into all the world and proclaim it to every creature,' how long do you think it would take to do it ? " One of these brave fellows, accustomed to obey orders without hesitation or delay, and at peril of life, promptly answered, " *Well, I think we could manage it in about eighteen months.*"

There are, perhaps, in round numbers one hundred million of Protestants in the world. Could each of that number somehow reach ten of the unsaved, the whole thousand million would be evangelized; and could each be brought to give one cent a day, our missionary treasuries would overflow with three hundred and sixty-five millions of dollars every year. Of course we cannot depend upon any such numbers in this work. Nominal Protestants include millions of mere professors, members of state churches, formalists and ritualists, and millions more who do not even profess to be disciples, and are openly immoral and infidel.

But let us suppose that there are *ten millions* of true disciples who can be brought into line, and who by systematic effort can be made to furnish men and money for this work, even *with this tenth part of Christendom the world may be evangelized before the twentieth century dawns.*

We are not responsible for *conversion*, but we are responsible for *contact*. We cannot compel any man to decide for Christ, but we may compel every man to decide one way or the other; that is, we may so bring to every human being the gospel message, that the responsibility is transferred from us to him, and that we are delivered from blood guiltiness. God will take care of the results, if we do our duty. We are to preach this gospel everywhere for a witness, not coldly, officially, formally, but earnestly, prayerfully, lovingly; we are to set up Christian churches, schools, institutions, homes, in the midst of pagan communities, as part of this witness to the power of the gospel; then, whether the gospel prove a savor of life or of death, our fidelity will not fail of its reward.

We repeat, that it is our solemn and mature conviction that before the close of this century the gospel might be brought into contact with every living soul; for if we could so organize and utilize ten millions of disciples as that every one should be the means of reaching with the good tidings one hundred other souls, during the lifetime of this generation all the present population of the globe would be evangelized; or if the sublime purpose should inspire the whole church to do this work before this century ends, each of this ten million believers has only to reach between seven and eight souls every year for the fourteen years that remain.

For many years the writer has been urging, both by tongue and pen, the necessity and feasibility of a grand campaign for Christ, with reference to the immediate occupation of all unoccupied fields, and the immediate proclamation of the gospel to every living soul; and after a wide discussion of the proposition by some of the ablest writers upon the subject of missions, the conviction is only established that the present crisis imperatively demands that the entire forces of the Christian church should be enlisted and engaged in this glorious work. A spirit of consecrated enterprise should apply to this giant problem the best and soundest business principles; a system should be devised which shall prevent waste of time, money, and men, and economize and administer all the available force of the Church. The imperial clarion of our Lord summons all his hosts for the great crusade.

Nehemiah was a model organizer. He built up the broken walls of the Holy City, and with a small, poor remnant of the people finished the work in fifty-two days. The perfection of his organization was the secret of his success, and it embraced three grand principles: first, *division of labor*, every man at work over against his own door; secondly, *co-operation*, all engaged in one work and operating upon one plan; thirdly, *concentration*, all at the sound of the trumpet rallying to defend any weak and assaulted point. Put those three principles into practice in the work of foreign missions, and we may build the wall of gospel witness around the world in a few years; we may push the advance of our missionary hosts so rapidly and systematically, that on every hill, in every valley, from equator to poles and from sea to sea, the gospel's silver trumpet shall sound.

Fifty years ago seven humble shoemakers in a shop in Hamburg undertook the work of evangelization on the principle of individual responsibility. In twenty years they had organized fifty churches, gathered ten thousand converts, distributed four hundred thousand Bibles and eight million pages of tracts, and preached the gospel to fifty millions of people. As they went from place to place, the work grew, and new converts inspired with similar zeal became helpers, so that a population as great as that of the United States, or of the Congo Free State, heard the gospel within those twenty years. If any are distrustful of mere arithmetic as applied to the problem of missions, here is a practical proof that it is perfectly feasible so to organize the work as to reach one hundred millions of people every year, and that, too, with only an insignificant Gideon's band.

CHAPTER XXXIV.

THE LABORERS ARE FEW.

HUMAN life is too brief and the field is too great for the Church ever to overtake the needs of the field, without a large increase of the working force. These thousand millions of unevangelized souls are dying at the rate of thirty millions a year, and as many more are coming on the stage of life. What can these few thousand workers do, themselves mortal, to meet the wants of such a mortal race? It is plain that what we are to do for our own generation we must do, while that generation lasts; and this is utterly impracticable, if not impossible, unless the Lord of the harvest, in answer to prayer, sends forth more laborers into His harvest.

We say, with hesitation, yet from the force of deep conviction, that, if we would largely increase the missionary force, we must in some way *lessen the time and cost of the preparation of the average workman.*

The gathering of funds is sufficiently slow, and the securing of volunteers sufficiently difficult; but the most formidable barrier to the work of evangelization is that, even where both men and money may be obtained, it takes too long a time and too costly a culture to train the average workman; and this one obstacle often overtops all others, and is practically insurmountable.

For example, a pastor whose heart and tongue are on fire urges the claims of a lost world, and there are a few who respond, " Here am I, send me; " but they are generally for the most part from the poorer and less-educated classes. The wealthy are often electro-plated with avarice, and our appeals ring upon a cold, hard, metallic surface; or worldly schemes and business pursuits have them in their coils. The cultivated sometimes drift into philosophic doubt, and sometimes are already engaged in the learned professions, or journalism, or other congenial work. The few dormant consciences that do awake under our appeal are generally found in persons to whom wealth and learning do not open attractive doors at home. How disheartening, when one such offers to go to those regions beyond, to be told at the outset that from five to ten years must be spent in preparation!

One instance, known to the writer, may stand for a large class. A young Welshman, found competent to exhort, was, after the fashion of the Welsh Methodists, licensed. Afterward, coming to America he found a home in one of our Presbyterian churches, where he was much esteemed for piety, capacity, and love for souls. He and his earnest wife came to his pastor and begged to be sent to a foreign field. But how was he to get a license? Though he was sound in doctrine, he had neither a classical nor theological training, and had no means to pursue a prolonged course of study. The most he could do would be to get, under his pastor, a training in theology, church history, and the English Bible. Unless some such shorter road to the mission field could be found, these two willing souls cannot carry out their heart's wish, and the field that needs workmen so much must lose two devoted laborers.

Some denominations, when called to confront such perplexities, cut the Gordian knot by putting such workers into the field. The Romanists clothe with garb, girdle, and crucifix, every willing and loyal servant of the church, and send such forth with a blessing. The Methodists license and even ordain those who are apt to teach, abating the severity of the demand for trained and scholarly men, in order to provide more average workmen. Spurgeon, working on an independent basis, sends out from his own college, in thirty years, nearly a thousand ministers, missionaries, and evangelists, after from one to three years of study. Pastor

Louis Harms trained raw recruits in his mission school, and, without any rigidly uniform system of training, sent colonies of workers to scores of new stations, encouraging every willing soul to do the work for which he was best fitted, and further fitting each workman for the proposed sphere of labor.

These are signs of the times that ought not to be undiscerned or unheeded. It is possible to hold fast to standards of qualification which are too severe, inflexible, inelastic; and to make the road too hard and too long by which laborers get into the harvest field. The solemn, weighty calling of the ministry ought not to be entered too hastily or easily; a high standard helps to high average attainment, and unduly to lower the standard may lower also the dignity of the office. All this we are ready cordially to concede, as also the demand of these days for trained men. But even this true principle may be pushed to an extreme; in avoiding laxity, we may swing to rigidity.

Trained men are everywhere needed, but it

is as leaders, planners, organizers; under and behind them, very many who have far less training may do excellent work. One master mechanic not only guides a score of common workmen, but stamps upon their work the impress of his own genius, taste, and skill; he, like Briareus, has a hundred hands, but all guided by one head. A few West Point graduates plan defences and strategic movements for the ordinary rank and file to garrison or execute. The ministry needs scholarly leaders, masterly organizers; but under a few skilled generals an army of volunteers may move, and carry the enemy's works by storm.

There ought to be a change in our ecclesiastical tactics; our system of training for the mission field must be more flexible and more economical of time and money, or we cannot send workmen into the great world-field in adequate numbers. Conservatism will counsel rigid adherence to antiquated custom, on the ground of jealousy for the sacred office; and justify a prolonged course of education as a severe sifting process, that separates the pure grain and leaves the incapable and irresolute to be blown from the threshing-floor like chaff.

At the same time, there are plain facts that, like storm-signals, fly in our face and bid us prepare for the crisis, even now at hand. On the borders of our own land, and in foreign lands, where our trained workmen confront vast vacancies which must be filled and strategic points which must be manned against the coming conflict, they are glad to set at work every man and woman that can be used. Men who have no college diploma, and could not furnish that supreme test of scholarship, the " Latin essay," if found capable, willing, and winning, are licensed and ordained. Abroad, native converts who show true piety and develop real capacity are authorized to preach, and set as pastors over native churches, with little or no special training except in the Bible. They are taught the Gospels as their " systematic theology," and the Acts of the Apostles as their "church history," and the sermons of Peter and Paul as their " homiletics," and the pastoral epistles as their " pastoral theology ; " and then put into the places of trust. The necessity of having more helpers, and of multiplying self-supporting churches and supplying them with pastors, compels those who are on the ground, and have control, to shorten and simplify the course of training.

Why should not the whole church adopt the same policy? The " rules " of our book are servants, and not masters, and should be made to bend, if necessary, to bear the burdens of mission work. Any system that is unduly oppressive, and that tempts us to evasions and irregularities, is no longer a harness, but a yoke, or a strait-jacket, and needs modification. It is the almost universal testimony of foreign missionaries that we are making a grave mistake in demanding of candidates a long and tedious preparation, irrespective of their capacity, circumstances, age, character, or prospective field and work. Facts show that scholastic training is not necessary for effective service. There are scores of heroic men doing valiant battle for the Lord and the faith, who were never in college or seminary. Native converts, sent out in apostolic fashion as lay-preachers to tell the simple story of the cross, are to-day making disciples by the hundreds in China. Let the church of Christ devise some safe way by which willing souls may get into the field and at work without this long, laborious, costly preparation, and we may within ten years double the number of missionaries in home and foreign fields.

Where men are going to foreign lands, a part of their training might be left to be secured on the ground, while engaged in the study of the languages of the people among whom they are to labor. Even those who cannot preach, but are willing to work, may help in teaching, Bible and tract distribution, translating, editing and printing, or even in manual labor, all of which are closely connected with missionary work. Dr. Crummell, himself a Cambridge graduate, after twenty years on the Dark Continent, pleads for *industrial training*. The superiority of Sierra Leone over Liberia, as prosperous and independent, building its own churches, supporting its own ministers, and contributing largely to missionary work, he attributes mainly to the fact that the slaves, rescued by English cruisers and placed there for safety, were taught trades and industries, and so became prosperous mechanics and merchants, and founded families whose children have gone to England for scholarly training.

We feel persuaded also that the Church should send forth not only individual preachers and teachers, but Christian *colonies*, to mission fields. Why not, in Salt Lake Valley, confront a hideous Mormonism with the witness of a Christian community, with consecrated homes, and workmen who abide in their calling with God? Why not send similar colonies into the Congo basin, to plant Christian churches and schools, to illustrate the divine idea of family life and good government, and in all departments of industry and the learned professions, exemplify the spirit of the gospel in the presence of hovels of polygamy, mud idols, and licentious indolence?

We advocate, without hesitation, a *new basis of training for mission fields*, a shorter course, and one more practical in character. Those who are to do good work, at home or abroad, should be sound in doctrine, familiar with the principles of New Testament church polity, and thoroughly trained in the *English Bible*. Then they might be sent to their fields, under control of trusted brethren, to do such work as they are fitted for, and spend the time that would have been spent at home in Greek, Latin, and Hebrew, in applying themselves to the languages they are to use in their fields, and to the study of the people among whom they are to labor.

This method would have this additional advantage, that it would so employ candidates in direct work for souls, as to keep their spiritual life warm and earnest. We have often observed that the seven years of our college and seminary life not infrequently leave candidates with a chronic chill. Long withdrawal from active work, and absorption in mere study, are not favorable to burning zeal. Intellectual standards often displace the higher spiritual ideals. If young men, in the ardor and fervor of their first love, could be promptly trained in the doctrinal and biblical basis of all true mission work, and sent to the home or foreign field to get at work for souls while they complete their preparation for their life-mission, not a few of our greatest missionaries have affirmed that immense gain would come to the work in energy and enthusiasm. The converted natives who are set working before their first love grows cold, never lose that first love. If volunteers could be encouraged to go promptly forward with preparations for the field, and, without tedious delay, placed in the field and at work, they would never lose the impulse and impetus of their present earnestness and enthusiasm; others would catch fire at the altar of their consecration, and we might find ourselves,

under the lead of Divine Providence, *inaug-
urating a new era in Protestant missions.*
It is plain that something needs to be done
beyond what is now doing; some new clew
must be found to the mazes of this missionary question; some new factor found
for the solution of the greatest practical
problem ever before the Church. What we
are to do, must be done quickly. The generation is passing away, and we with it.
These millions of unsaved souls we must confront at the bar of God. What can we do
for their salvation, — nay, for our own salvation from blood-guiltiness, — before the sun
of life shall set?

CHAPTER XXXV.

MEETING THE CRISIS.

THE field is the world, and the church is the recruiting office for workmen. The great disproportion between the immense masses of the unevangelized, and the available resources of men and money and means from which the working force must be drawn, makes the utmost economy necessary. The Church has comparatively few who can be relied on to supply consecrated workmen or consecrated capital for this vast work; and yet we are positively wasting both men and money by the rivalry of several denominations in the same fields, while other fields are entirely unoccupied.

Dr. Murray Mitchell said, a few years ago, that it is a disgrace to Protestantism, that only eighty years since, the mission work in the regions beyond was systematically inaugurated; and it is still a burning disgrace to the church of Christ that the millions of Protestant church-members sustain in the foreign field not over ten thousand men and women, and contribute not over ten millions of dollars yearly, while in Scotland alone the Presbyterian Church has more than three thousand ministers.

How little do we appreciate the fact or the extent of the unoccupied fields. Anam, with twenty millions; Kurdistan, with three millions; an immense tract of the Dark Continent lying north of the equator; the vast Congo basin, touched as yet only on its edges, with fifty millions more; Afghanistan, with eight millions. Thibet, Mongolia, and Arabia have recently been embraced in the great missionary girdle; but only a beginning has been made, and we might properly include them among the unoccupied fields. Only fragments of the vast populations of China, Africa, South America, have even come in *contact* with the gospel.

The Greek and papal churches hold three hundred millions under an almost unbroken spell of ignorance and superstition. There are one hundred and seventy millions of Islam's deluded followers, and while Christian missions have scarcely approached them, they are themselves making new converts to the False Prophet; in China alone, one hundred thousand proselytes to Mohammedanism are reported as the result of a recent aggressive movement. Meanwhile, every year a vast host, equal to the entire population of the United States, passes into eternity.

The destitution of the great countries where missions are most thickly planted is still appalling. When, in 1881, Mr. Stevenson, of the China Inland Mission, travelled through China from east to west, he journeyed *sixty-one days*, over more than *a thousand miles*, from Bhamo in Upper Burmah, to Chun-King in the province of Chuen, without finding one mission station between those points; and that awful shadow thus unrelieved by any gospel light was a thousand miles broad, as well as long, for on either side of his line of travel stretched a territory five hundred miles in breadth, with only *one station*, Kwei-Yang, in its whole extent. In a word, here was a square of territory one thousand miles long and broad, embracing one million square miles, thickly populated, and three mission stations, two of them on its extreme borders and one between. It is far better now; but even now the provinces of Kan-Suh and Kwei-Chau each has three missionaries for its three millions; Shen-Si has ten missionaries for ten millions; Yun-Nan, four missionaries for six millions. Here are four provinces, together nearly four times as large as Great Britain and Ireland, and twenty two millions of people,—but only twenty Protestant missionaries.

At such a rate, the church of Christ, we repeat, can never overtake the unevangelized population of the earth. Yet our Lord meant no absurdly impracticable project when He said, "Disciple all nations." It would be easy for a consecrated church promptly to carry the banner of the cross to the ends of the earth, to furnish all the workers needful, and to make the missionary treasuries overflow. If one Christian woman can herself disburse two millions of dollars in benevolence; if one Congregational deacon can appropriate a million to missions; if twenty persons in one year can together give nearly four millions, — what might not one hundred million Protestants give, if only a *tithe* were honestly and systematically laid on God's altar?

England paid for the war in Afghanistan sixty millions, while one eighth of that sum was all the entire church of Christ could devote that same year to the evangelization of the heathen, the world-wide campaign for Christ. As Dr. William Ashmore says, "Whiskey is the stand-pipe in our comparative expenditures;" it shows how much money there is now spent for one article of harmful indulgence, that might be spent for missions, without touching our actual necessities or comforts; and the whiskey level is *nine hundred millions* annually.

The internal revenue tax on tobacco in New York alone in 1879 exceeded seven millions of dollars. How true it is, as Rev. F. T. Bayley says, that "a deified appetite outranks a crucified Christ."

For liquor and tobacco two hundred and fifty-five times as much is annually spent as for missions; or taking together with these, bread and meat, sugar and molasses, iron and steel, lumber, cotton and woollen fabrics, boots and shoes, and public education, every year there are spent in these various directions *six hundred and seventy-five dollars to every dollar given to foreign missions.*

As we could give money without feeling it, so we could give men. Our late four years' war not only required rivers of treasure, but rivers of blood, — five hundred thousand lives were sacrificed to save the Union. Yet we give to the heathen world ten thousand men and women, and can do no more, gathering them from the whole church of Christ. The missionary band has been called " heroic ; " and it is. Gideon was brave ; but even after his force was reduced from thirty-two thousand to three hundred, he had one man to every four hundred and fifty of the foe. But, as Dr. Ashmore says, if Gideon's band had been reduced to the same proportion as the missionary band to the millions they confront, he would have had less than one man to the hundred and thirty-five thousand Midianites.

Can anything be done to meet this present crisis? The writer of these pages begs those who are praying for the coming of the kingdom to consider the following suggestions, in addition to those already made.

Let a great council of disciples be called to consider the question of the world's destitution, and to confer as to its speedy evangelization.

At some great world-centre, like London or New York, or at Rome, the old heart of the papacy, or at Constantinople, the golden gate to the Moslem empire, or at Jerusalem, the very city of the great King, let an ecumenical council be summoned to meet, as early as practicable, and let every evangelical Christian denomination be represented by commissioners clothed with authority; and at such a council let three things be done: —

First, let workers from every mission field be there, like Paul and Barnabas on their return to Antioch from their first mission tour, to "rehearse all that God has done with them, and how he has opened the door of faith to the nations." Let them present that huge mass of facts which shows that, since the world began, no half-century of history has been so full of stupendous and startling interpositions of God as the last fifty years of modern missions. In the mouth of many witnesses let every word be established; and let it be shown that from the Pillars of Hercules to the Golden Horn, from the Arabian Gulf to the Chinese Sea, from the silver bergs of Greenland to the Southern Cape and the Land of Fire, God has flung wide the ports and portals of sealed empires and hermit

nations, hurled to the very ground the walls
and barriers of ancient customs and creeds,
made all nations neighbors, and woven into
unity the history and destiny of the whole
race by the shuttles of traffic and travel. Let
all men face the fact that no outlay of men,
money, and means ever brought returns so
rich and rapid as the mission enterprise;
that even the seeming waste of precious
lives has been but the breaking of the
costly flask, filling the world with the odor
of unselfish and heroic piety, and prompting
to its imitation. Let the Hawaiian group,
first-fruits of the sea unto God, send her
witnesses; let Syria, whose soil is sacred
with Jesus' blood, tell of her Christian
schools and printing-presses; let Madagascar witness the power of the gospel that has
made her God's angel sounding the trumpet
of grace at the eastern gate of the Dark Continent; let the Pacific Archipelago tell of the
thousand churches that point their spires like
fingers to the sky; let the witnesses gather
from India, where the " Lone Star " has

grown to a constellation of glories; from Japan, striding in seven-league boots toward a Christian future; from Italy and France, just coming forth from the sepulchre of the Dark Ages, bursting the bonds of a thousand years of priestcraft and superstition!

The church of Christ is asleep. Let a thousand trumpets, like the sound of many thunders uttering their voices, rouse us all from apathy and lethargy. Let facts, like the fingers of God, write God's message on the walls of our temples of mammon and palaces of luxury, as in letters of fire, till selfishness and worldliness shall tremble at the manifest presence of the Lord!

Secondly, *let the whole world-field be mapped out*, divided and distributed among the evangelical denominations of Christendom. To prevent waste and friction, and apparent division of forces in the face of a gigantic and united foe, let right of priority be conceded to those who are already working successfully in any field, and let the one purpose and motto be occupation of fields now destitute, and the speedy evangelization of the world. Let there be a careful adjustment of the boundaries of each field, and agreement as to the principles of mutual co-operation and comity.

The monks of the Middle Ages, who went forth in companies of twelve, electing one of their number as captain, taking possession of the regions beyond for Christ, set us all a grand example; and inspired by Judson Smith's enthusiasm, the Oberlin band was recently formed upon this principle, and have gone forth to occupy the province of Shen-Si, in China.

Thirdly, let there be a proper distribution of the forces, so as to use all workmen as economically as possible. It is a shame to us not to husband all our resources, where the demand and the supply are so disproportionate. As others have magnanimously retired from Turkey, leaving the American Board to concentrate its energies on that field; as Syria and Siam are left mainly to American Presbyterians, and Egypt to the

United Presbyterians: so, where any existing missionary force is adequate to the work, let others retire from the field and go to some other, unprovided for. Above all, let there be no strife between those who are brethren, but let a magnanimous charity abound. We are not sure that it would not be wise and practicable to appoint a general board of supervision and control, representing various co-operating bodies of Christians, and having power to act in their behalf. What is desirable is, that in some way all unoccupied territory shall be assigned to those who shall feel responsible for it, and that those who supervise the work shall thoroughly understand the needs and comparative claims of each part of the wide field, and act with integrity, impartiality, and charity. Why not, in these days of business schemes that are colossal in capital, magnificent in plan, and world-wide in their extent, — why not undertake the King's business as something that requires haste, and should summon to its prompt prosecution every loyal disciple!

CHAPTER XXXVI.

A WORLD'S MISSIONARY COUNCIL.

HE suggestions, modestly put before the great brotherhood of fellow-disciples, by one comparatively obscure believer, in the preceding pages, are a simple but earnest contribution to the solution of the greatest problem ever submitted to the church of God. However crude they may seem, they are the result of a quarter of a century of constant thought and study upon the missionary problem. In part, they have already been put into print in fragmentary forms, from time to time, and have been met with friendly discussion and cordial approbation from others who are interested in the same great end, the evangelization of the world.

The proposition of a World-Council has especially been received with wide and emphatic favor. For example, a beloved representative of the great Methodist Episcopal Church,[1] echoing the need of complete and " thorough organization, and of one great, all-comprehensive plan and purpose, and of persistent, concerted, and concentred movements and assaults upon the strongholds of the powers of darkness," suggests that such a world's missionary congress be called, that it be composed of delegates both from the ministry and the membership of the churches, representatives known to be unusually wise, pious, and missionary-spirited; that they be clothed with authority to act and vote according as their own wisdom and the manifest leadings of the providence and Spirit of God may dictate; and that similar workers from all the fields of mission work give such congress the benefit of their presence, experience, and counsels. He further suggests that such delegates be chosen at

___

[1] Rev. J. M. Driver. Missionary Review, VIII. 464.

least one year in advance of the assembling of the Council, and that similar councils might follow at longer or shorter intervals of from one to five years, as the exigencies of the work might require.

From none of the friends of missions, however, have more enthusiastic responses come than from Mr. Robert Arthington, of Leeds, England, who has been so liberal in his benefactions to missions, especially in Africa. In personal letters, both to Rev. R. G. Wilder, editor of the " Missionary Review," and to the author of this volume, he expresses his warm and hearty approval of the proposition of a World-Council. He writes as follows : —

" The Church Missionary Society of London has lately held a large number of open meetings simultaneously over England, to promote the missionary enterprise. At one of these meetings, on February 11, 1886, I moved the following resolution, promotive of universal evangelization : —

RESOLUTION.

" 'This meeting, deeply sensible that far greater missionary effort is needed in order to fulfil the parting command of Christ to His disciples, resolves that the time has come to map out the whole world in portions, in its heathen parts, and allot it amongst all missionary societies, — whose aim it is to give a whole Bible to a whole people, — thus enlarging the fields already occupied, and giving new spheres to each society, so as to cover the entire globe.

" ' And further it is resolved, that a request be sent from this meeting to the committee of the society originating these conferences, asking that they will confer with the various missionary societies in Europe and America, with a view thus to map out the world, and devise, by mutual suggestion, a plan for general adoption.' "

He further says, emphasizing the matter as one deserving very prayerful consideration:

" I feel quite sure that good to all eternity must come of this movement. Would not the occupation of the whole world simply for evangelization by the Word of God be greatly to His glory? I judge it would not be difficult to make prayerfully the proposed apportionment of the unevangelized parts of the world. . . . If we do not attain all we could desire, it would be a great advance to have made the apportionment. Who can doubt that the plan, if accepted and carried out, would lead to an amazing increase of missionary effort and success! Any one might still be free to preach the gospel in any part of the world; but for economy of time, strength, money, and forces, all might be entreated not to establish missions in parts assigned to others and occupied by them. I shall be glad to assist in counsel and correspondence."

As this is a utilitarian age, and the question will be asked, whether any good would be likely to come of such a World-Council, not equally to be secured by existing agencies, we venture to add, that certain results of the highest importance would be almost certain to follow.

1. First of all, the very spectacle of the gathering of the representatives of evangelical Christendom, for the sole purpose of the speedy evangelization of the world, would exceed in sublimity any event from Pentecost until now. It would awaken joy in heaven as well as in earth.

2. It would mass the great facts of missions as they have never been massed before. The

testimony would be so universal, as to be irresistible in its cumulative force. The members of the Council, overwhelmed by the witness from the world-wide fields, would return to their homes to scatter the holy fire, — to diffuse information, to arouse the Church to its responsibility, and to kindle inspiring and contagious enthusiasm. The press would be called into requisition to multiply and scatter the reports and proceedings, and the Council would have a trumpet-voice whose echoes would be heard round the world.

3. We might look for results of the highest practical value in the proper distribution and apportionment of laborers, and the prompt occupation of every part of the field. A holy emulation would take the place of sectarian rivalry. The assignment of particular fields to particular denominations, and even to individual churches, would intensify interest and quicken the sense of responsibility. A practical, economical mode of administration would commend itself to business men, and it would bring ampler contributions to God's

treasury. Men and women would be more ready to offer themselves to the work.

4. The impression of substantial Christian unity would be invaluable, both in quickening our home co-operation and in promoting the success of our missionary labors. As Macaulay says, " Where heathen unite to worship a cow, the differences between Christian sects dwindle into insignificance." It is the reproach of missions that several denominations are needlessly occupying the same fields, while other fields have not a missionary of any sort.

5. Best of all, we should confidently expect the Lord himself to acknowledge such a council of disciples by a new effusion of the Holy Ghost. Two results would be involved in this,— a spirit of prayer for missions, and a spirit of personal consecration to the work. Without these, all our methods and measures are but so much machinery without an adequate motor. We are deeply and unalterably persuaded that the whole progress and success of the work of missions depend upon

a wide-spread, radical revival of primitive piety. There is too little prayer, and hence too little of the power that comes by prayer. Give us Elijah with his face between his knees, in seven-fold supplication, and we shall have the cloud like a man's hand, and then an overspread sky and a mighty rain.

In the summer of 1885 there was issued by the Convention of Believers at Northfield, Mass., an appeal to fellow-disciples to engage in concerted prayer. It was printed in circular form, and sent far and wide. It has found its way to every part of the world by the aid of the million-tongued press. This year, at the Summer School for Students held at Mount Hermon, Mass., where nearly three hundred young men from about one hundred colleges gathered for four weeks of prayer and Bible study, the spirit of missions was marvellously poured out. Early in the meetings it became evident that a new and strange influence was at work from above. There had been perhaps a score of those young brethren who came on the ground with the mission field in view. But when, on August 1st, the farewell meeting was held, *one hundred* of those students had consecrated their lives to the work of missions, and had chosen four of their number systematically to visit the colleges of the land and seek to enkindle a holy zeal for the work of a world's evangelization. Those who were present at both the Convention of 1885 and the Summer School of 1886 were constrained to say, " This is the finger of God." It was obviously the work of no man, but of His Holy Spirit; the prayers which for a year have been ascending to God from disciples of every name, for a new effusion of the Holy Ghost, are beginning to be visibly and gloriously answered.

In view of all these facts, and in hope and faith of wider co-operation among praying believers, and a more general and sympathetic union and communion in believing supplication directed to this great end, we bring this little volume to a fitting close by appending to these chapters a copy of the Appeal, believing that nothing but such a new outpouring of the Spirit in answer to prayer will enable the church of Christ properly to meet

THE CRISIS OF MISSIONS.

A WORD SUPPLEMENTARY.

———◆———

AS the missionary voice which sounded from Northfield last year has resounded in so many echoes, we give it a new chance to be heard, by the humble aid of this book.

AN APPEAL TO DISCIPLES EVERYWHERE.

ISSUED BY THE NORTHFIELD CONVENTION.

To Fellow-believers of every name, scattered throughout the world, Greeting:

Assembled in the name of our Lord Jesus Christ, with one accord, in one place, we have continued for ten days in prayer and supplication, communing with one another about the common salvation, the blessed hope, and the duty of witnessing to a lost world.

It was near to our place of meeting that, in 1747, at Northampton, Jonathan Edwards sent forth his trumpet-peal, calling upon disciples everywhere to unite in prayer for an effusion of the Spirit upon the whole habitable globe. That summons to prayer marks a new era and epoch in the history of the church of God. Praying bands began to gather in this and other lands; mighty revivals of religion followed; immorality and infidelity were wonderfully checked; and, after more than fifteen hundred years of apathy and lethargy, the spirit of missions was re-awakened. In 1784, the monthly concert was begun, and in 1792 the first missionary society formed in England; in 1793, William Carey, the pioneer missionary, sailed for India. Since then, one hundred missionary boards have been organized, and probably not less than one hundred thousand missionaries, including women, have gone forth into the harvest-field. The Pillar has moved before these humble laborers, and the two-leaved gates have opened before them, until the whole world is now accessible. The ports and portals of Pagan, Moslem, and even Papal lands are now unsealed, and the last of the hermit nations welcomes the missionary. Results of missionary labor in the Hawaiian and Fiji Islands, in Madagascar, in Japan, probably have no parallel even in apostolic days; while even Pentecost is surpassed by the ingathering of ten thousand converts in one mission station in India within sixty days, in the year 1878. The missionary bands had scarce compassed the walls and sounded the gospel trumpet, when those walls fell, and we have but to march straight on and take possession of Satan's strongholds.

God has thus, in answer to prayer, opened the door of access to the nations. Out of the Pillar there comes once more a voice, " Speak unto the children of Israel, that they go forward." And yet the church of God is slow to move in response to the providence of God. Nearly a thousand millions of the human race are yet without the gospel ; vast districts are wholly unoccupied. So few are the laborers, that, if equally dividing responsibility, each must care for at least one hundred thousand souls. And yet there is abundance of both men and means in the church to give the gospel to every living soul before this century closes. If but ten millions, out of four hundred millions of nominal Christians, would undertake such systematic labor as that each one of that number should, in the course of the next fifteen years, reach one hundred other souls with the gospel message, the whole present population of the globe would have heard the good tidings by the year 1900 !

Our Lord's own words are, " Go ye, therefore,

and disciple all nations;" and, "This gospel of the kingdom shall be preached in all the world for a witness unto all nations; and then shall the end come." Peter exhorts us both to "look for and hasten the coming of the day of God;" and what if our inactivity delays His coming? Christ is waiting to "see of the travail of His soul;" and we are impressed that two things are just now of great importance: first, the immediate occupation and evangelization of every destitute district of the earth's population; and, secondly, a new effusion of the Spirit in answer to united prayer.

If at some great centre like London or New York, a great council of evangelical believers could meet, to consider the wonder-working of God's providence and grace in mission fields, and how fields now unoccupied may be insured from further neglect, and to arrange and adjust the work so as to prevent needless waste and friction among workmen, it might greatly further the glorious object of a world's evangelization; and we earnestly commend the suggestion to the prayerful consideration of the various bodies of Christian believers, and the various missionary organizations. What a spectacle it would present both to angels and men, could believers of every name, forgetting all things in which they differ,

meet, by chosen representatives, to enter systematically and harmoniously upon the work of
sending forth laborers into every part of the
world-field!

But, above all else, our immediate and imperative need is a new spirit of earnest and prevailing
prayer.   The first Pentecost crowned ten days of
united, continued supplication.   Every subsequent
advance may be directly traced to believing
prayer, and upon this must depend a new Pentecost.   We therefore earnestly appeal to all fellow-
disciples to join us and each other in importunate
daily supplication for a new and mighty effusion
of the Holy Spirit upon all ministers, missionaries, evangelists, pastors, teachers, and Christian
workers, and upon the whole earth; that God
would impart to all Christ's witnesses the tongues
of fire, and melt hard hearts before the burning
message.   It is not by might nor by power, but by
the Spirit of the Lord, that all true success must
be secured.   Let us call upon God till He
answereth by fire!   What we are to do for the
salvation of the lost must be done quickly; for
the generation is passing away, and we with it.
Obedient to our marching orders, let us "go into
all the world, and preach the gospel to every
creature," while from our very hearts we pray,
"Thy kingdom come."

Grace, mercy, and peace be with you all.

Done in convention at Northfield, Mass., August 14, 1885, D. L. Moody presiding.

Arthur T. Pierson, Philadelphia, Presbyterian, *Chairman.*

A. J. Gordon, Boston, Baptist.

L. W. Munhall, Indianapolis, Methodist.

Geo. F. Pentecost, Brooklyn, N. Y., Congregationalist.

Wm. Ashmore, Missionary to Swatow, China, Baptist.

J. E. Studd, London, England, Church of England.

Miss E. Dryer, Chicago Avenue Church, Chicago.

Committee.

University Press: John Wilson & Son, Cambridge.

BOOKS ON MISSIONS